Marooned on Mars

A Science Fiction Novel

Marooned on Mars

By LESTER del REY

Jacket Illustration by Paul Orban

Endpaper Design by Alex Schomburg

Cecile Matschat, Editor
Carl Carmer, Consulting Editor

THE JOHN C. WINSTON COMPANY
Philadelphia • Toronto

To

EVELYN

Tomorrow's World

Most of us will live to see pictures of the Moon— pictures taken by men who actually walked on the surface of that round ball in the sky! Twenty years ago, a rocket weighing a few pounds could travel a few hundred feet at most; now, rockets weighing a few tons travel several hundred miles. From that it is only a short step to building rockets that weigh hundreds of tons and can travel the 239,000 miles to the Moon. This will be in the world of tomorrow!

Rocket-driven ships, of course, can travel where there is no air. We know that by actual proof; the less air around a rocket, the better it performs. We also know a great deal about how the ship must be designed and what will be found on the airless Moon when we get there. We've never seen the other side of the Moon, but we can be sure it's about the same as the side we do see. We can even guess how the Moon will prove useful, scientifically and commercially. We will probably establish a permanent base there, even though it will be incredibly expensive.

From there, we will move on. Once we've learned

the secrets of the Moon and how to build even better rocket ships, we'll look toward the other planets—Mars, Venus, and the moons around Jupiter.

Mars will probably be the first planet explored. Venus is nearer, but Mars has always aroused more interest. Unlike the Moon, Mars seems to have air, water, and *life!* In our telescopes, we've seen the ice-caps around the poles melt with the coming of spring, and we've noticed that the red planet then begins to turn green. In the fall, this green turns to the shades of autumn leaves on Earth, behaving as if it were living vegetation.

We don't know whether there is animal life there. But it seems possible that the same conditions which produced plant life may also have produced animals of some sort, just as such conditions produced both plants and animals on Earth. There may be some form of strange insect life, for instance, or moving, crawling life of a type we can't imagine—but we can't know without going there. We can't even say that intelligent life is impossible.

Once, some scientists believed there was proof of intelligence on Mars. A lot of speculation was given to the mysterious "canals" of the planet (though the word "canals" is a bad translation of the Italian *canali,* which means "channels"). These can be seen as straight lines on a map of Mars, crisscrossing the surface. Unfortunately, we still don't know much about them. We don't even know they really are so straight, or that many of them aren't simply tricks played on the tired eyes of the observers.

For a long time it was believed that they were great trenches, dug by the Martians—and that would have indicated a high degree of intelligence there. Then doubts began to grow. Photographs didn't show them, and the later, bigger telescopes showed them less plainly than the smaller ones. Some people, in fact, never had been able to see them. Hence, a few years ago, science began to believe that there were no canals after all.

Today, this has changed. The latest photographs show some of them as mere fuzzy markings, hard to trace, but definitely there. Some of them seem to come and go; old ones disappear and new ones appear from time to time; modern maps don't entirely agree with those made half a century ago. But the markings on Mars are real, even though there isn't enough water on the whole planet to fill such "canals."

We still know very little about them. They *may* be evidence of intelligence, but certainly no intelligent life on Mars can have reached our stage of civilization. The thin air—thinner than the air on top of the highest mountain on Earth—would make fire impossible. Without fire, men would never have come out of the caves to begin smelting metals. Fire was man's first great tool and metals his second; without such tools for a start, a high level of civilization wouldn't have a chance. Probably the canals are only some natural phenomena which have nothing to do with intelligent life.

We can't know for certain until we go there and see for ourselves. Since we've always been a highly curious form of life, we'll make the long trip there to find the answers at the earliest possible moment.

This is an account of such a first trip as it *might* be made. The technical details are generally accurate and nothing here is really fantastic. We can already write about such a voyage across millions of miles of space without the need of too much wild imagination. When the accounts of the first real trip are made, sometime in the future, we can be sure they will read something like this fictional one. And it doubtless will be much sooner than many of us imagine.

L. D. R.

Contents

CHAPTER   PAGE

    Tomorrow's World vii
1. *Return to Moon City* 1
2. *Rocket Ship Eros* 13
3. *The Wrong Birthday* 24
4. *Stowaway to Mars* 35
5. *All Hands to Control* 46
6. *Meteorites!* 58
7. *Mars Ahead* 71
8. *Crackup Landing* 83
9. *A New World* 95
10. *Marooned on Mars* 108
11. *Eyes in the Night* 121
12. *The Mysterious Canals* 134
13. *On Guard* 145
14. *Welcome Mat* 156
15. *The Martians* 167
16. *Lost in the Caverns* 178
17. *A Dying Race* 189
18. *Martian Gesture* 200

Chapter 1 Return to Moon City

FOR the last hour, the big helicopter had been climb-
ing through the night and the thinning air toward
the peaks of the Andes. Now, 18,000 feet above
sea level, it straightened out and the sound of its
motor settled down to a steady hum. Sunlight was
already touching the mountaintops, and the rocket
field showed up plainly, only a mile ahead.

The stocky, blond boy in the passenger seat stirred
suddenly and began rubbing sleep out of his blue
eyes. Chuck Svensen was short for his age—not quite
eighteen and only five-feet-seven—and there was no
sign of hair on his face yet. He had always had trouble
convincing people he was as old as he was, and the
eagerness on his face as he saw the rocket field
made him look even younger. But there was respect on
the pilot's face.

"Must feel good to be going home to the Moon,"
the man suggested with a touch of envy in his voice.

Chuck grinned. "Great. After four years up there
at one-sixth Earth weight, I feel like a ton of lead
here. But it was worth it!"

1

"Worth it!" The pilot snorted, and the envy was stronger this time. "Kid, you're one of the six luckiest guys alive. I'd give my right arm for a chance to go on that first rocket to Mars!"

Chuck nodded. It still didn't seem real to him. For four long years he'd watched the ship being built for the journey, without any hope. Even when the Governor at Moon City had won his request to have some-one chosen from the Moon group as one of the crew, Chuck had hardly dared to dream. The age limit was set rigidly between eighteen and twenty-seven, and he would be barely eighteen when the date of the take-off came. When his experience with radar and his physical fitness finally won the chance for him, he'd been the most surprised person in all Moon City.

Then had come long nights of study with almost no sleep, a special trip to Earth, and two weeks of grueling tests to prove his ability. Now he had passed, and was on his way back to the Moon—to leave almost at once for Mars!

The helicopter was settling down on the rocket field. Chuck could see men moving about in the heavy clothing required by the bitter cold; the air was too thin for comfortable breathing, and all wore masks that supplied extra oxygen and made them look like in-human monsters. He adjusted his own mask as the helicopter touched earth, hovered, then slipped onto the field.

The special little rocket ship from the Moon had already landed and was being readied for the trip back. From the three fins at its base, which now served as legs, it stretched up about forty feet to a sharp tip: the whole looked something like a fat cigar equipped with stubby wings. Pumps were busy piping liquid into the fuel tanks and loading cranes were storing boxes of precision tools into the little freight compartment. One huge machine had pulled out the worn lining of the big rocket tube at its tail and was fitting another in place, while a second was working on the ship's compact atomic motor, replacing the original cans of plutonium with fresh ones.

But Chuck had seen all that before. He shoved through the men who were guiding the machines at a safe distance from the opened atomic engine, and headed toward the canteen. In his clothes and mask, he looked like any of the others, and no one paid any attention to him. It was a welcome change after the publicity he had received when he had passed his tests.

Inside the pressurized dining hall, Chuck found the little rocket pilot busily consuming coffee and watching the counterman make more. Jeff Foldingchair stood less than five feet tall, but his deep-tanned face and blue-black hair fitted his claim to being a full-blooded Cherokee Indian. The man had been on the second trip to reach the Moon, twenty-five years before, and he was still one of the best rocket pilots in the business.

His black eyes met Chuck's in the mirror behind the counter. He didn't look around, but his white teeth flashed in a sudden smile. "Pull up, kid, and have a coffee. Sure is good to drink real Java after that concentrate stuff on the Moon. We've got ten minutes before we blast off . . . um-m, congratulations. Everybody in Moon City's proud enough of you to bust!"

"Banana cream pie," Chuck ordered, dropping beside Jeff. On the Moon there was food enough, and plenty of fresh vegetables from the tank gardens; but this would be his last taste of the luxuries for a long time. "I'm lucky you're here, Jeff. I thought I'd have to take one of those slow ships back—and nine hours beats four days any time!"

Jeff shook his head, motioning for more coffee. "No luck to it, kid. Governor Braithwaite sent me down to pick you up. The tools I'm hauling back were just an excuse; they could have waited. Chuck, you never saw such a celebration . . ."

He stopped as a uniformed attendant came through the tunnel that led to the main offices. The man motioned to the pilot, and Jeff got up with a shrug and followed him out.

Chuck smiled to himself as he attacked the pie. He could imagine the celebration in Moon City when they heard he had passed. No real nation could ever be more intensely patriotic than the little Lunar colony. It didn't matter that he'd been born in the United States and had only been there four years; nationalities didn't matter there—a year was enough to make a real Moon citizen. Esperanto, the artificial language which had been used at first to avoid the confusion of many languages, was now the normal language, even in the homes; nobody asked about a man's birthplace— it was enough that he was now living on the Moon.

There was even some talk of independence in the

future, though everyone was well enough satisfied with Governor Braithwaite. He'd been appointed by the United Nations, which controlled the whole Moon, but he was as much of a Lunar citizen now as anyone else who lived there.

The Mars Expedition, of course, was being run by the United States under special charter from the UN to use the Moon, and the Governor had no real authority over it. Yet his general popularity had led to a quick acceptance of his request for one crew member to be from the Moon; and nobody had questioned his choice of Chuck for the position. He'd exceeded his authority in sending the speedy little rocket for Chuck, but the boy knew nobody would protest.

Jeff came back, interrupting Chuck's reflections. The sharp planes of the pilot's face showed worry, though he grinned at Chuck. "Meteorites out in space—they may change the course to Mars a bit," he reported; the worry was in his voice too. "Eat up, Chuck, we're about ready to make the big jump."

"Dangerous meteorites?" Chuck asked. Most of the bits of rock and metal in space called meteorites were tiny things, but they traveled so rapidly that they could easily damage a ship.

Jeff shrugged, "Hard to say. Um-m, I've been thinking, though. Maybe this business of going off to Mars now is all darned foolishness. Ten years from now, it'll be routine; maybe you'd be smarter to stick with your family, let some other fool go chasing after new planets."

"Jeff!" Chuck dropped his fork onto the half-finished

pie and swung around. "What's up? Is something wrong with my permit to go?"

Jeff shook his head and handed over the radargram. "They've just decided to move the take-off to Mars ahead two days. Forget it, I guess I'm just nursing a grouch today. Let's get going."

Chuck knew better than to try to pump the man. He got up and put his mask on again. But the worry persisted. There was no reason for Jeff to start advising against his going, unless there was a good chance he couldn't go. The pilot had been one of the men to recommend Chuck to the Governor. Yet the radargram had said only what Jeff had indicated. Either there was another 'gram, or he missed the obvious.

On the field, the shields had been put back over the rocket ship's atomic engine, making it safe to climb the ladder to the control room. Those shields had been developed slowly over the last quarter-century until they were nearly perfect. Half an inch of such shielding was better than fifty feet of solid concrete in holding back dangerous radiation. Without them, atomic-powered rockets would have been too dangerous to use. The old chemical rockets had needed a hundred tons of fuel to get two or three tons to the moon. Now the little six-ton rocket was powered by a mere two tons of liquid in her tanks.

Chuck followed Jeff up the ladder and into the tiny air lock, waiting while Jeff locked the outer door. They went through the inner one, which Jeff also locked, and up through a small hatch into the pilot's quarters. The pilot went through the routine of checking the valves which controlled their air supply. Then he dropped onto a soft sponge mattress on the floor and began fastening himself down with web straps.

Chuck did the same. Lying down, the human body could take more acceleration pressure than in any other position, and all take-offs were made while they were stretched out at right angles to the direction of flight. All the control buttons and levers were set into the mattress directly under the pilot's hands.

On a panel overhead, needles told what was going on in the ship; a big chronometer measured out the passing seconds. "Ten seconds," Jeff announced.

Chuck forced himself to go limp on the foam rubber. Jeff nodded tautly and pressed a single button.

The big rocket jet behind let out a sudden bellowing roar that rose to a screech and faded out a few seconds later, as they passed the speed of sound. The floor seemed to come up and slap at Chuck's back. Under the pressure of four gravities of acceleration, his weight seemed four times that on Earth. His chest labored under the effort of breathing, and the blood roared in his ears, trying to run back from the front of his body. His eyes pressed against their sockets, and everything blurred. Even Jeff was gasping, in spite of his long experience.

They were adding 128 feet to their speed each second—going from zero to a full five thousand miles per hour in one minute, and adding the same amount to their speed with every minute that passed. They were already beyond Earth's atmosphere, and still the rocket exhaust thundered out behind.

If there had been heavy air around them, its resistance would have heated the ship to the melting point and wasted most of the thrust of the rocket. That was why the ships still took off from the highest possible point on Earth, where the air was thinnest.

Mercifully, the pressure lasted only a few minutes. Jeff's fingers tripped the switches, and the rocket-jet ceased. The ship had gained more than the seven-miles-a-second speed needed to carry them away from Earth and it would coast the rest of the way. Earth's gravity still pulled at them weakly, but since it pulled against the ship exactly as strongly as it did against the two men, there was no feeling of weight or pressure against the ship's floor.

The rebound of the mattress threw Chuck up against the straps, and his stomach did a series of flip-flops under the change. For a few seconds, his head spun dizzily as he lost his sense of balance. He'd been sick for hours on the first trip to the Moon, but his body had learned to adjust. Now the waves of sickness passed. It was almost like floating in clear water, without the wet sensation.

For a moment, he was tempted to undo the straps and go floating about, bounding from walls and ceiling with a mere push of his finger. Then he remembered that he was no longer a child, and relaxed back beside Jeff, watching out through the observation ports.

There wasn't much to see. The rear radar screen overhead showed the Earth shrinking behind, while the Moon was still a tiny, sharp ball of white in the black sky. The stars were mere pinpoints of bright, cold fire; there were more than could be imagined on Earth. The sun lay to one side, but an automatic filter protected their eyes, and made it seem only an irregular circle of leaping flame. It was the same view Chuck was used to seeing from the airless Moon.

Jeff pointed to the side, and Chuck turned to look. A few miles away, one of the old doughnut-shaped orbital stations floated. It circled above the Earth in an orbit, like the Moon, but nearer, and might go on forever. Before the new fuels and improved shields had made atomic-powered jets possible, men had used the stations as a step toward the moon; now they were abandoned, except for a few scientific uses.

"Progress," Jeff said. "Used to take twenty trips from Earth to a station before we could get enough fuel for a ship to leave it for the Moon. Now we do it directly. They built them to use for atom-bombing enemies on Earth in case of war; but when too many countries got orbital stations up, everybody got scared, and they turned the whole thing over to the UN. Started out for war and they led to real world peace!"

Chuck had studied it in school, though he found it hard to believe that the United Nations Council had ever been weaker than the countries it now ruled so easily.

Jeff took one final look as the station shot out of view. Then he relaxed beside the automatic timer that would waken him, closed his eyes, and was soon snoring quietly. Chuck tried to do the same, but the feeling of weightlessness bothered him, reminding him of the first trip, and the four years that had passed since then.

Chuck had always dreamed of leaving Earth, but he'd never seen a rocket take-off or spoken to a man who'd left the planet until he was nearly fourteen. His father had been head engineer for a small company in the Midwest, and Chuck had been forced to content himself with what he could read about the Moon ships. Then, without warning, his father had announced that he was chosen to work on the big ship being built on the Moon to reach Mars. Chuck had nearly gone wild at the idea of actually living on the Moon.

When the novelty had worn off, he'd pestered the construction men into letting him help during his free time away from school. It had seemed enough to be able to help in making it possible for others to go farther to other planets. His mind traced the days and months of watching the ship grow, and his eyes slowly closed.

They were almost to the Moon when Jeff wakened him. Chuck saw that the ship had already been turned around with its tiny steering rockets, and now had its jet pointing toward the Lunar surface. In the rear radar screen, the big crater named Albategnius showed he was almost home. The crater's eighty-mile diameter almost filled the screen, and the two smaller craters inside it stood out clearly. Moon City lay in the smaller one that the first explorers had nicknamed Bud, and the Mars Expedition construction was going on in the other, known as Junior. Around the flat crater, the rim walls that rose for thousands of feet were already shutting out the rest of the Moon, while the central peak seemed to stick straight up toward them. Even the observatory building beside it could be seen.

Jeff nodded sharply, and cut in the big rocket-jet to slow their rushing speed. Landing was like take-off, except that it was trickier, since they had to reach zero speed exactly at the moment they touched the surface. Jeff frowned into the screen, and juggled the controls, while the agonizing pressure again caught at Chuck. When it ended, there was hardly a jar as they settled down on the three landing fins.

"Sweet landing," Chuck said, and Jeff nodded. It had been an exceptionally smooth one.

They waited, while the ground below cooled from the heat of the rocket blast. Then there was a tapping sound from the surface of the ship. Jeff fingered a control that would open the outer air-lock door, waited, and sent a signal to close it again. The lock permitted men to enter the ship from the vacuum outside without too much loss of the ship's air. A moment later, the inner door opened, and Chuck's father pushed up the hatch to the control room.

He was wearing a suit that looked like a diver's, with a transparent globular helmet over his head, which he now threw back. In his arms were suits for Jeff and Chuck. His tanned face broke into a wide grin, and his big, booming voice seemed to shake the little room.

"Chuck! Boy, you look like a million. Welcome home!"

"Hi, Dad!" Chuck's throat caught as his father

grabbed him in one arm, squeezing him briefly. Then
he grinned back. "I passed! Dad, I can go to Mars!"

The smile slipped from William Svensen's face, and
his eyes darted suddenly toward Jeff Foldingchair.
The pilot avoided the look and shrugged helplessly.
"I told him the ship would take off two days early,"
he said uncomfortably. "I figured he knew when his
birthday was. Oh, heck, Svensen, I couldn't really tell
him!"

Chuck dropped back weakly toward the mattress.
He'd been a dope not to know what it meant. Nobody
could leave on the ship for Mars until he was eighteen
and Chuck's birthday was one day after the new
take-off date.

Svensen shook his head slowly, and one hand
fumbled out toward his son, holding the suit. "Maybe,"
he said slowly, "maybe we can do something about
it. Here, get into your suit. Your mother's waiting at
home, and we'd better get going. We'll talk it over
later. Nobody has said you can't go yet."

Chuck hid his head as he fumbled with the suit,
trying to keep his father from seeing the sudden tears
in his eyes. He knew the older man didn't think he
had a chance!

Chapter 2 Rocket Ship Eros

O N the Moon's surface, the sun was blazing down mercilessly, heating the rocks underfoot beyond the boiling temperature of water. Only the heavy suits and the helmets which cut off all but visible light made walking possible. Chuck and his father left Jeff behind and headed toward the edge of the smaller crater, where Moon City lay. Here where gravity was only one-sixth that of Earth, their normal walk was a series of twenty-foot leaps that carried them along at better than ten miles an hour.

In the absence of air, no speech was possible, and Chuck was glad of it. He wanted time to recover from the shock of finding all his hopes were ruined. He followed his father silently, letting his eyes study the inky shadows and glaring high lights of the Lunar landscape.

They skirted the small group of storage sheds and receiving buildings, from which trucks were heading out toward the rocket ship, and came to the little cogwheel tracks that led down into "Bud." The electric-powered car was waiting at the stop when Chuck

13

halted for a quick look down into the little crater. Being away for even a few weeks made it all seem new again.

There wasn't really much to see. Moon City had been built like the cities of the old cliff-dwellers. The living quarters were hollowed out of the crater rim, well back from the surface. Outside, only a half-dozen air-lock entrances showed, leading into tunnels that served as streets and connected the few shops and the homes. Such construction protected them from the occasional falling meteorites, and enabled them to live without space suits most of the time; the air that was baked from chemicals in the rocks was sealed inside.

All the dwellings were grouped together. Deep in the walls of the opposite side lay the big atomic generators that furnished all their power, and the chemical laboratories and high-vacuum plants were near by; here almost zero absolute temperature could be had in any shaded section, and a nearly perfect vacuum lay all around them. Such industries were the backbone of their trade with Earth.

Even their food was grown underground in tanks containing water and chemicals, and these hydroponic gardens were lighted artificially. Sunlight was missing for fourteen days and then was much too intense for the next fourteen. It was easier to regulate fluorescent lighting.

Svensen tugged at Chuck's hand, and the boy climbed onto the little tramcar. Two other men in suits had already boarded it—José Ibañez from the loading sheds and Abdul ibn Hamet, who worked in the uranium mines—the only uranium deposit discovered on the Moon. Both grinned warmly, and the Arab bent forward to touch helmets with Chuck, so that his words could be heard.

"Bonan vesperon, amiko," he greeted. The moon operated on a twenty-four-hour day, in spite of its twenty-eight Earth-day period, and Chuck realized it was already afternoon to them. *"Domaĝo, iu ne?"*

Chuck thought it was more than a shame as he returned the greeting. The starting of the little car cut off further comments, though, and he breathed a sigh of relief. He was in no mood to discuss his bad luck with anyone yet. He was glad when the two men moved off toward the garden entrance after the car stopped.

Half a mile away, the entrance to a small one-man air lock marked the "apartment house" where the Svensens lived. Chuck lagged behind, half-dreading the questioning of his eight-year-old sister, Kay. At the lock, he let his father go first, waited until the green light indicated the lock was clear, and followed uncertainly. When he passed the inner door, his father was stripping off his suit and storing it with the others in the lockers along the walls.

"I told them no party tonight," he told Chuck, as the boy began removing his own suit. "I knew you'd want a little peace. And, Chuck—don't worry; we won't talk about the trip for a while. Right?"

Chuck met his father's understanding glance, and

his voice choked a little. He should have known how
they'd take it. "Thanks, Dad. But tell me, what *did*
happen?"

"The observatory spotted a small swarm of meteorites that would intercept the ship's course part way to
Mars. They had to refigure it to avoid that, and it
worked out best if the ship left two days sooner. So
you lost. The charter is pretty stiff about the age limits,
but Governor Braithwaite is pulling strings, and he
may be able to get it stretched that much. After all,
they have to have a radar operator. . . . Come on,
supper will be cold."

The apartment was on the same level as the tunnel,
and they moved toward it. Chuck saw that the door
was already open. He let out a yell, and a small, furry
dog suddenly shot out at him, wriggling and leaping
all over him.

"Tippy! You old rascal. Miss me?"

"Went crazy looking for you," Svensen answered.
The little dog had been smuggled to the Moon when
he was just a puppy by Jeff Foldingchair two years
before, to become one of the six dogs on the Moon.
Growing up there, he took Lunar conditions for
granted; in fact, he even had a small space suit, complete with a sleeve for his tail. But he still acted like
any other dog whose master had left him too long.

Then Chuck's mother was hugging him. Tears were
running down her plump, pleasant face, but she only
kissed him once quickly, before rushing back into the
little kitchen. His sister was dancing around, her shrill
voice cutting through the sound of Tippy's barking.

"Didja bring me a present, Chuck? Did ya, huh?"

Chuck located a small box of carefully wrapped chocolates and a second later her mouth was too full for further sounds.

He turned into his own room to clean up. It was just as he'd left it, with a thin coating of dust over the mess of home-built radar apparatus that filled most of one end and had been his hobby since their arrival here; it must have bothered his mother, but she'd left it undusted, as he'd asked. The only change was an acknowledgment card from an Earth station he had contacted just before leaving.

He was home, no question about it. He tried to tell himself that Jeff was right, and only a fool would want to leave this. But he couldn't make himself believe it. He hardly tasted the dinner his mother had so carefully prepared.

In the morning, he was still awake when he heard his father getting ready for work. Automatically, Chuck gathered up his work clothes and began dressing. They ate hastily and went out through the air lock, where a little electric tractor was waiting with the other men who were going on the early shift.

The little tractor carried them onto the cogwheel tram which climbed slowly up to the surface. Then it sped out across the bottom of the big crater toward Junior. There was no tram there to take them down, but an inclined ramp had been built, and they moved down that.

The big rocket ship was nearly completed. The scaffolding had been pulled away, and it stood upright on its three leg-fins. Fully fueled, it would weigh nearly thirty tons by Earth weight—about five tons on the Moon. It stretched upward to a height of nearly a hundred feet. Unlike the smaller rockets, this looked something like a huge flying oil tank. It was sixty feet in diameter at its base, its wings were tiny things, and the point rounded out bluntly. With only the very thin atmosphere of Mars to be fought, it didn't need streamlining.

The outer skin was complete, down to the name—*Eros*. All the main parts inside had been installed. The atomic engine lay above the big rocket tubes; then came the fuel tanks, the hydroponic gardens, and finally the crew quarters and control room. Only a small amount of work remained.

Chuck turned up to the control room, leaving his father, who was supervising adjustment of the engine. The radar equipment was still in need of work, and the boy had been doing a large part of the installing of that.

Big Richard Steele, the trip engineer, was already in the control room, testing the air circulation. Chuck barely closed the main hatch as the man threw over the valves. Air hissed in, and the two threw back their helmets.

"Hi, Chuck." The engineer had the rich voice with which many Negroes are blessed. His face was streaked with sweat that glistened against the walnut-brown of his skin, but the lines of fatigue only deepened the calm sureness of his expression. He sniffed the air that was circulating, and nodded approval. "I've been here all night getting the raw paint smell worked out, but it's okay now. Might as well enjoy a little breather outside our helmets. How's the boy?"

"Fine, Dick—I guess."

"You guess? Oh, that! Well, you're going, if the rest of us have anything to say. We had a powwow with Governor Braithwaite as soon as we got the news. Didn't we get you picked for the trip?"

"This is different," Chuck pointed out. "This is a charter rule."

The big man nodded slowly. "Yeah, I know. But I haven't heard that they've appointed anyone else, and we aren't going without a radar operator; you can bet on that. This ship is meant for six men, and it's going to leave with all six. Better close up—I'm pumping the air back."

Chuck reached for his helmet snaps as the air began thinning out. Steele watched the meters. Then he slapped Chuck's back, and went down the hatch.

Chuck studied the charts of progress made and then began soldering, feeling slightly better. He couldn't believe there was much chance, but the fact that the others wanted him along killed some of the hurt.

Then the routine of the work took up his thoughts. Soldering was always a pleasure without air to corrode the cleaned surfaces of the metal. There might be disadvantages to living on a world with no atmosphere, but it had its compensations.

The second shift man relieved him eventually. He touched helmets with Dick before taking over. "Governor wants to see you, Chuck. *Bonan sancon!*"

Chuck found Governor Braithwaite expecting him. The man was almost the perfect picture of a beardless Santa Claus, with a beaming face and a hearty manner that was completely genuine in his case. Now, however, there was concern and worry behind his quick smile of greeting.

"*Bonan tagon*, Chuck. I'd have seen you last night, but I knew you'd be tired. I'm deucedly sorry about all this, you know. Now I've got a little good news for you—not much, but something, at least."

Chuck waited, while the Governor fished through his papers. "Oh, bother. Never mind, I know what it said." He tossed the papers aside, and leaned back. "You're an important young man. The President of your United States has made an official request for the UN to let you go. You made the highest rating of anyone who took the tests for the position, and Earth agrees with me that we on the Moon shouldn't be neglected. If we can speed up action in the Council, we may get that blasted rule waived yet."

"You shouldn't have taken so much trouble," Chuck began.

The Governor cut off his protests with a wave of his hand.

"Bosh. I'd have a rebellion on my hands if I didn't, son." He shook his head slowly. "But I'm not going to give you any false hopes. It will be difficult—very difficult. If we can stall them off in selecting someone else, and if we can cut through enough red tape in the Council, we have a slim chance. The chief trouble is that the next highest man is a young fellow from the United

States of Chinese ancestry; naturally the Council's
Chinese Delegate will oppose us."

"Just how much chance do I have?" Chuck asked.

"I wish I knew. I'd sleep better if I did. But chin up,
son! We'll do everything we can. And there's an old
law I can invoke to quarantine the appointee for medical inspection and inoculation. If we don't get a replacement for the crew tomorrow, I'll be able to hold
him until after the ship leaves for Mars."

"You wouldn't!"

"Wouldn't I?" Governor Braithwaite chuckled, and
came around the desk to clap Chuck lightly on the
shoulder. "I'm a quiet man, Chuck, but just a bit stub-
born. You go on home now, and let yourself sleep like
a young heathen. We're all fighting for you."

Going down the long tunnel toward his home, Chuck
thought it over, and tried to feel that it was now on
the laps of the gods. But it was the very uncertainty
of his chances that bothered him the most. He stopped
at a store to pick up the little newspaper that came out
each day and scanned it carefully. Two freighters had
come in that day, but there were no passengers. His
replacement hadn't come yet. Then he grinned at his
own foolishness; if the man had arrived, Governor
Braithwaite would have known about it first.

There was no news that night that he could find by
using his radar set. He tossed and turned in his bed,
telling himself that quarantining his rival would be
an unfair trick, and that he should refuse to take advantage of it. But the fact that he had proved himself
to be the best man for the job opposed that; it wasn't

fair to the rest of the crew to take second best, he kept
thinking.

In the morning, going to work, he scanned the bul-
letins hastily. The Council was meeting, but a question
about the order of procedure had taken up all the day
before, and Braithwaite's appeal hadn't even been
mentioned. His eyes looked at the shipping notes.
There were no freighters due for the day, and no passengers had come on the late night ship.

At the *Eros*, men were still working, but there was
very little left to do, and they weren't worrying much
about that. Men clustered together in little groups,
touching helmets and conferring busily. Chuck
couldn't take their stares. He went up into the control
room and shut the hatch behind him.

It was only half an hour later when the rich baritone
of Dick Steele reached him through the air that now
filled the ship. He opened the hatch.

"News, Chuck. Jeff Foldingchair was pulled down
to Earth on emergency orders last night. He's just
landing back here now. We'll know what's up in a few
minutes."

Chuck nodded. He should have known that the
Earth administrators would anticipate the Governor's
trick and make sure the replacement was here in plenty
of time. He put his tools away neatly.

"I'm going home, Dick."

"I'll ride you back," Dick suggested. He snapped
down his helmet and went down with Chuck.

The men pulled back to let them pass. Chuck's
father was one of the few men not in sight, but he

stuck his head out of the engine hatch and waved as Chuck climbed onto the tractor. Everyone was trying to look casual, as if nothing were happening, but they all knew what it meant.

Chuck paused to take a long look at the big rocket ship before he nodded for Dick to start the tractor. In the sky overhead, he could barely make out the tiny dot that was Mars. It seemed farther away than it had ever been before.

Chapter 3 The Wrong Birthday

CHUCK'S mother met him at the door, and her face was filled with worry for him.

"You've got company, Charles," his mother told him. "I sent the young man into your room. I didn't want you to be bothered."

Chuck tried to smile at her. He nodded and went into his room.

The young man sitting there looked more uncomfortable than Chuck. The light olive complexion and the definitely Chinese eyes of the visitor showed the reason; Chuck's replacement was not only on the Moon, but in his own room!

The stranger stood up awkwardly and held out a hand. "I'm Lewis Wong, Mr. Svensen. I guess you know why I'm here. I—I just want you to know I think it's a dirty trick. That's why I came here the first thing."

It took Chuck by surprise, and he fumbled for words, but the other went on quickly.

"I saw the figures on your tests, and you're the man for the job. Anyhow, you had it first. So I hope your Governor's appeal goes through."

"I thought it had been turned down," Chuck cut in.

"No—not when I left. They hadn't gotten to it. I'm here just in case they do turn you down. Look, Mr. Svensen, I learned how they feel about you up here—your friend Foldingchair made that clear. I . . . nice radar set you have there. I . . . oh, doggone it all, I mean, I can refuse to go, can't I?"

Chuck turned it over, feeling as awkward as the other looked. He wondered what he would have done, had the situation been reversed. But he had to make some answer. "Suppose they picked me and I refused to go," he began.

"Yeah." Wong nodded, his eyes on the floor. "Yeah, I guess I wouldn't want the position then much, either. It was just an idea. What do they call you—Chuck?"

"Except for my mother. She doesn't like the nick-name, though I guess she's used to it. Hey, Lew, how'd you like to come out to the ship with me tomorrow? It's about done, but I can sort of help you get the feel of things. It makes this stuff look pretty sick."

They began to discuss Chuck's rig then; Lew apparently knew more theory than Chuck, though he'd had less chance to practice with the super-long-range sets. This set had been one of the leading arguments in Chuck's favor, since he'd built it out of worn or rejected parts from the big set at the receiving station and had erected his own beamed antennas. The testing board had commented openly on the fact that it

showed he could improvise—and improvising might
prove important on the long journey.

"Where are you staying, Lew?" Chuck asked finally.

Lew shrugged. "I don't know—I supose they've assigned me rooms, but I came here first, as soon as I'd
registered. Why?"

"That means you'll be quartered with one of the
crew. Why not stay here, instead? After supper, I can
heat up the rig and we'll try a few calls to Earth. Hey,
Mom!"

Mrs. Svensen agreed readily enough, as Chuck had
know she would. If she was surprised, she didn't show
it. That night Chuck slept in the same room with the
man he'd been almost hating the night before. He lay
awake for some time, thinking about it. It would have
been so simple, if Lew had proved to be unlikable;
now he couldn't even hope for the Council to decide
in his favor without worrying about the blow it would
be to the other.

Yet, strangely, he felt better in a way. Having someone almost his own age to talk to had taken some of
the pressure off him. He began planning the next day,
until sleep finally clouded his mind.

As it turned out, though, they didn't get to the ship.
The next day the decision came from the Council.

Living on the Moon, Chuck had forgotten other
things. He had learned to accept all men and all
nationalities as equal, but there were still traces of
racial jealousy on the mother planet. Seven nations
had joined with the United States and Governor

Braithwaite in asking for Chuck's exemption from the charter rule, but China remained adamant.

The delegate from the Chinese Republic was honest about it. Chuck, he admitted, was better fitted in some ways, and it was a very nice idea to have someone from the Moon on the ship. But other promising candidates had been turned down because of their age—some only a few days from that required. One of them had been of Chinese stock, though a citizen of the United States, like Lewis Wong.

Caucasians had reached the Moon first. Now it was only fair that a descendant of China be among the first to reach another planet. The delegate regretted the hardship to Chuck, of course. But he could only refuse, both in justice and in loyalty to those of his race, to have anything to do with changing the rules.

China cast her vote, and under the rules only a unanimous decision could change the charter. Chuck Svensen would not be allowed to make the trip to Mars.

"Jingoism," Lew Wong said hotly. "I'm no more Chinese than Dick Steele is African. I'm just plain American, Chuck, like you. When the United States voted against me, why couldn't they let it stand?"

Chuck's father shook his head slowly. "No, Lew. No more jingoism than the idea the Moon should be represented. There's nothing wrong with being proud of your race—and that's all the Chinese delegate was doing. You can't blame him. If Chuck can't go, then he can't—and I'm glad you're the one to take his place."

Chuck was glad his father had said it. The shock of hearing the verdict had left him speechless for a moment, even though he had been fairly sure of what it would be.

He grabbed Lew's hand and shook it, without knowing quite what he was saying. He didn't even hear his new friend's lame excuse for leaving, and was only half-aware when Lew left.

William Svensen stood up slowly, tamping out the ashes from his pipe. It had been almost as much of a blow to him as to Chuck.

But his voice was calm enough as he began putting new tobacco into the pipe. "Tough luck, kid. By the way, Vance and Rothman are testing the *Eros* tomorrow. Vance told me today he was going to see you get the first chance at her, no matter what happened. So you'd better get to bed. You'll need a clear head for the test."

"Lew should make it," Chuck protested weakly. "He'll need the experience. I guess—"

The phone cut him off, and his father picked it up. "Sure, Doc . . . What? . . . Look, he was feeling fine a few minutes ago. . . . Oh . . . we'll be there!"

He swung around to Chuck quickly. "Lew just reported in to Medical. Doc Barnes says it looks like appendicitis. Says the boy claims he's been bothered ever since he got up here."

"It's a fake, Dad."

"Of course it is. Fool kid. Come on!"

Doctor Barnes met them inside the infirmary and led them into his office. There was a little smile on his sharp-featured face. "Looks like you'll have to go, Chuck," he began.

Svensen cut him short. "Doc, you know Lew Wong has no more appendicitis than I have. If you're just playing along with it so my boy can go in his place, you're making a mistake. I'm not going to permit it! Chuck won't go; the Council says he can't, and that settles it. They'd only send someone else, anyhow."

"But—" The doctor's face purpled for a second. Finally, he nodded. "I guess you're right, Will. It seemed like a good idea, but it wouldn't work. Um-m-m. Still, Wong just *might* have a touch of chronic appendicitis that shows up under a gravity change; in that case, I'd be risking his life if I didn't forbid his going without a full examination and consultation. If he insists he feels sick, my hands are tied."

"How about symptoms?"

"He's either read up on it—any good encyclopedia would do—or he has something. There's no fever, though, and his pulse is normal."

Svensen lifted an inquiring eyebrow toward Chuck, then nodded. "Okay, son, get in there and change his mind. And if you can't, I'll do it with a hairbrush!"

Lew was sitting on the cot in the little receiving room, smiling faintly. As Chuck came in, he dropped back and began groaning.

Chuck stared at him. "I'm not going, Lew. Even if I wanted to replace you, Dad wouldn't let me. If you want to hold up the ship while they find someone else, you can. But you can count me out. I'm not

even going on the test flight. That's your job. Thanks
for the try, but it's no dice!"

He swung about sharply and went out, closing
the door before Lew could argue with him. It was
only a minute later that Lew followed him, looking
sheepish.

"I guess you think I'm a complete fool," he admitted.
"Okay, it was just an idea that didn't work. But you're
going on the test flight, Chuck."

The doctor reached for the admittance card and
began tearing it up. The other three started back
toward the Svensen home, with Lew still trying to
convince Chuck that he should make the test hop.

But Chuck had decided. He'd had enough of half-
hopes and plans that didn't amount to anything. There
was no sense in teasing himself with something that
could only make him envy Lew the more.

"I'll be watching you," he finished. "From the surface here. But if I can't go to Mars, I'm too old to
play games. It's your job, Lew. And that's that."

"And what about you?"

Svensen dropped his arms over the shoulders of the
two boys. "Chuck will want to learn piloting under
Jeff Foldingchair—Jeff asked about it when I talked
to him last night. Eighteen's the right age for that too.
And when the next rocket goes to Mars—well, I'm
betting the other pilots won't have a chance against
a Moon boy who can pilot and run a radar set to boot.
Right, son?"

"Right!" It had been Chuck's wish once, though
he'd never hoped to get his mother's permission to

attempt his own piloting. But she'd never go against his father's promise. He grinned at Lew. "There'll be other trips, chum."

Behind them, someone had been calling excitedly, but they had been too busy to pay attention. Now in the momentary silence, Chuck heard his name. He turned, to see the Governor's male secretary racing toward them. "Governor Braithwaite wants to see you at once!"

"The council changed their minds?" Lew exclaimed.

"No, no." The secretary frowned. "Of course not. But they have made another decision. In fact, the delegate from China sponsored it. The news just came in."

They followed him, trying to get more information out of him, but he was enjoying the mystery and refused to tell any more. After the cat and mouse game of the last few days, Chuck had stopped reacting. He wasn't going to get all he wanted, but he'd still do all right. Just being part of Moon City was something worth being happy about. That, plus a chance to become a rocket pilot, was enough. He couldn't really kick. Going to Mars was something like going to heaven—and most people had to die to do that.

Probably the Council had decided to make some official apology to him, or to grant him full adult status on the Moon, with the right to hold an official job. It would be nice enough, but it wouldn't be important.

Governor Braithwaite was beaming happily as they entered. He shook Chuck's hand warmly, muttering something about how sorry he was that his appeals had failed. But there was something else on his mind, obviously, and he wasted little time in getting down to it.

"Chuck, you've no idea how much those ratings of yours impressed the Council. They were up for hours of consideration before the vote, you know. I tell you, it isn't every day a young man can take up that much time in the United Nations! They've decided you're being wasted here. Look!"

He handed Chuck a long transcript of a radargram, and stood beaming while the boy read it. Chuck skipped the formal part, until he came to the point of it:

At the request of the Delegate from the Republic of China, it is therefore resolved that Charles Svensen, now a resident of Moon City, shall be granted a Council Scholarship, as provided in the Act establishing the Committee for Educational Allocation. This Scholarship shall be for the period of six years at any university of his choice duly approved, to lead to a degree of Ph.D. in physics with any branch of electronics as a major study. During this time, Charles Svensen shall be considered a candidate for Council Advisor, and shall spend three months of each year at the behest of the Council in attendance at the Council meetings in the capacity of a Junior Advisor, for which he shall receive a recompense of $7,000 per annum, minus costs of tuition.

There was more official stuff, but Chuck had seen enough. He handed it back to the Governor. "That means they want me to take a course in electronics for six years and then go into United Nations work—research, I suppose?"

"Precisely." Governor Braithwaite beamed harder than ever. "You know, that's a remarkable resolution, Chuck. The Council absolutely shouted when the Chinese Delegate proposed it. They've only granted the full honor like this eight times in history, you know."

"What about it, Dad?" Chuck asked.

His father shrugged. "It sounds like a fine opportunity—better than I could ever offer you. If you want it, take it. You'll make more than you will piloting rockets."

"And have to give up the Moon as well as Mars," Chuck said. He shook his head. "No thanks. Governor Braithwaite, you can fix it up in fancy language. Just tell them I don't feel I can accept, and that I prefer to stay right here on the Moon!"

Braithwaite's face fell. He rubbed his hands together, and stared at the rug under his feet. He shuffled his papers about nervously. "I'm afraid I can't, Chuck." Again he shuffled the papers. "You see—dash it, you *can't* stay on the Moon. The Council never dreamed you'd refuse. They've already sent orders for me to pick up your Lunar permit within two weeks—and you know you can't stay here without one."

Chuck knew that; getting onto the Moon was something like being cleared for entrance into one of the most secret laboratories on Earth, only harder. Even Tippy had required a special permit, after Jeff had brought him out.

"And—" Governor Braithwaite cleared his throat, as the shocked look deepened on his face. "And it takes two years after a permit is picked up before you can apply for anything but a visitor's one-week stay, you know. That's part of the original Moon charter. Of course, you could appeal—though why you'd want to, I'm sure I don't know. But the delegates are human, after all, and they might feel insulted."

He forced his face into its usual cheerful expression. "Besides, think of the opportunities, Chuck. Why, you're one of the luckiest boys in the world. There's no telling how far you can go. Think it over tonight, and you'll see. You'll see."

Chuck had already seen enough. Sure, it was an honor, and he was grateful for their intentions. But the Council had never been off Earth, and they couldn't know what they were doing.

They'd promised him Mars and they were taking even the Moon away from him.

Chapter 4 Stowaway to Mars

U. S. 954090

THE area around the *Eros* was bathed in floodlights the next morning, and half of Moon City had turned out to watch the test flight. The Moon had swung about on its orbit until all of Albategnius crater was in darkness. Now one of the big searchlights swung around to follow a little tractor that came toward the ship, bearing five figures in clean, new space suits.

Captain Miles Vance, pilot Nat Rothman, and Lew Wong, of the crew, would make the test. Jeff Folding-chair, dressed in a slightly oversized suit designed for the crew doctor, was going at the request of the Space Commission, since his experience might be needed in an emergency. The fifth suit was worn by Chuck. It had come out from Earth before the Council's decision, and was too good to waste. There was even a tiny radio in the helmet which would enable him to talk with the others wearing similar suits.

Now Captain Vance's voice sounded in the headphones. "Still time to change your mind, Chuck."

"No." Out of habit, he shook his head inside the helmet. "I'm not going as supercargo. Anyhow, Mom didn't like the idea of my being on the test, so I promised her I wouldn't. She still thinks the ship may crack up, unless the test proves it to her."

He snapped the little switch in his glove, cutting off any further conversation, and jumped off the tractor to join the crowd. People were already moving back out of the danger area.

Chuck hadn't even wanted to watch the test, but now some of the crowd feeling seemed to reach him. The tractor went on to the ladder leading up to the ship's air lock, and his eyes followed the four figures up and into the ship.

Another helmet touched his, and he turned to see the Governor. *"Bonan matenon,* Chuck. Feel better now?"

Chuck tried to grin. He still felt the same, but there was no use blaming the Governor or making him feel worse.

"I guess so," he said. "But I'd still rather stay on the Moon."

"Um-m-m. Well, you know, I even sent out feelers to Earth—but they're going ahead with plans for you. Cheer up, boy, you'll enjoy the university life. It's just taking a little time to get used to the idea."

Chuck nodded again, and drew back into the crowd. The Governor had grown up when airplanes were the glamorous machines, and couldn't know what it was like to be born with a yearning for space and other worlds.

Now the crowd was drawing back faster. Chuck found a position where a convenient rock gave him a seat, and dropped onto it. The *Eros* sent a tentative spurt of shooting flame from its tubes, leaping two feet off the surface. It settled back, while meters were being read and compared with expected figures. Then the floodlights blinked twice, and the crowd tensed.

This time the flames from the rockets were a deep purple that seemed to etch the ground out from under them; the sound traveled through the rocks, and set up vibrations in the soles of Chuck's boots. The huge ship jumped from the ground like a race horse leaving the post. It leaped a hundred feet, five hundred, a mile, almost before Chuck could raise his neck to follow it.

Then it was only a hot, blue speck in the blackness of the sky. It continued for a full minute, before the flame vanished as the drive was cut. Chuck waited, knowing they were turning the ship over to blast against its direction and slow it. Finally, the blueness appeared again, but soon stopped. Now the ship would be drifting back slowly toward the Moon, while they checked the performance and again turned its rockets to point downward.

It was nearly twenty minutes before the blast shot out again, and the speck turned into a ship. Rothman's piloting was less sure than Jeff's would have been. The ship came to a halt fifty feet above the surface, and he had to take an extra blast to settle it, after the original cut-off. But it still was a good landing.

The test was obviously successful.

There was a buzz in Chuck's ears, and he cut his radio back on, to hear Jeff's voice. "Chuck! Stick around, will you? I'm leaving these boys to their figures, so I'll walk back with you."

Chuck acknowledged it, and moved as close to the ship as he could. It was nearly ten minutes before the ground had cooled enough for Jeff to come out. The pilot indicated the tiny aërial on his helmet, and jabbed twice. Chuck moved his switch away from the common channel for all the suits to second position, where he could talk to Jeff in privacy.

"How'd she handle?" he asked.

"Like a dream, kid. She's big and fat and built like a tub, but she has a lively set of heels. Now, what's all this about your being shipped back? You're no desk-jockey. I thought your father and I had it all fixed up for you to turn pilot!"

Chuck located a small tractor and started it toward the other crater as he tried to explain things to Jeff. The pilot grunted in disgust at the stupidity of all men who couldn't appreciate the lure of the rockets. But he agreed with the Governor.

"Once your permit's lifted, you're sunk. They'd call you an ungrateful puppy if you appealed it; anyhow, Braithwaite has to keep them happy if we're to get a bigger appropriation to set up a second colony. His hands are tied."

"I know it. I'm not blaming anyone, Jeff. But it doesn't make me any happier."

"Nor your Dad. I guess he wanted you to go as much as you did. Your family got used to losing you for a couple years on the Mars hop, but they don't like getting along without you for something you don't want. Look, how about coming over to my place? I picked up a couple of mincemeat pies; they got crushed a bit, but they're edible."

Chuck wasn't hungry, even for pies, but he didn't feel like going back to his own room and moping. He nodded, and they turned toward the entrance to the bachelor quarters. Jeff's room was filled with books and relics of the early rocket days and it was surprisingly comfortable.

Jeff sliced the pies, beginning a long story about the early trips he had made. In spite of himself, Chuck found himself listening. It was late afternoon before he finally stood up to go.

Jeff walked down the tunnel toward the Svensen apartment with him. "It's quite a ship, that *Eros*," he said suddenly. "More room. You could hide an army in the hydroponic gardens. If I were a little younger and crazier, I'd have sneaked aboard some night, like that young fool I was telling you about on our fifth trip up here. She'll be gone about two years and it'll be some trip. Hey!"

Chuck looked up at his shout. "What, Jeff?"

"Just hit me. You'll probably get your permit back about the time the *Eros* returns. At least you can get up to see her come in." They reached the apartment, and he turned to go. "Look me up before they ship you back, kid."

Chuck found his family already seated at the table, discussing the new work Svensen would be doing in the high-vacuum labs, now that work on the *Eros* was finished. But his father dropped it as he came in.

"The Governor fixed it for you and me to watch the take-off from the radar building," he said. "That way we can follow what goes on. In fact, I wouldn't be surprised if you get a chance to handle communications."

Chuck knew it should cheer him up, but his head was too full of the last words Jeff had said. He dropped into a chair. "Thanks, Dad. But—well, I've been thinking maybe I won't watch the take-off."

"Oh!" Quick understanding ran over his father's face. "Okay, son, just as you like." He went back to the details of his new job.

Chuck played with his food, trying to eat, but the new idea that had hit him was taking all his attention. He finished as quickly as he could and stood up. His mother was shaking her head over the food he had left, and he kissed her quickly. "I guess I'm just tired. I'm going to bed."

"I won't wake you in the morning, Chuck," his father promised.

It fitted perfectly with the idea, Chuck thought. He shut the door behind him, and dropped onto the bed. Then, because his family might look in on him, he climbed in, clothes and all, and pulled the sheets up to his neck.

It would take two years to get his permit back; but by then he'd be too far along with schooling to quit, and he'd still have four more years to go on Earth. If he had been going on the *Eros*, though, he could get a permit when he returned—and there'd be no strings. His father wanted him to go, anyhow; even his mother had approved of the trip. It wasn't as if he'd be useless; the examinations had proved his fitness for the trip.

He tried to remember Jeff's story of the boy who'd stowed away on the early Moon rocket. Jeff couldn't have known what he was saying. But the idea wouldn't leave. Of course, the Council would be angry; but in two years they'd forget—and they wouldn't deny a new permit to anyone who'd been on Mars!

He tossed about, trying to plan some way to get aboard the ship. Suddenly he realized that his mind was made up—he was going! They weren't going to turn him into a humdrum research man back on Earth after he'd been all set to explore the mystery of other planets. He'd stow away!

He waited, listening to the sounds of the family. It seemed to take an endless time to wash the dishes, put them away, and then discuss things—probably worry about him. He wondered how his mother would take his running off; then he remembered that her father had run off to join the Air Force, and that it was one of her chief sources of pride. She'd understand—and his father would be secretly pleased.

There was a final stir as they prepared for bed. He heard his mother's steps at his door, and quickly feigned sleep. A shaft of light touched his face. Then the door closed, and he heard the door to the main bedroom shut.

He waited another half-hour to be safe. Finally, he got up and turned on his writing light. The note was an awkward one—he knew he couldn't say what he wanted to. But it would have to do. He sealed it and addressed an envelope; it wouldn't be picked up until morning—or delivered until after the *Eros* had left.

He tiptoed out through the door into the tunnel— and almost stumbled over Jeff Foldingchair.

"Hi," the pilot greeted him. "You'd better get some spare clothes, kid. It's a long ways to Mars!"

Chuck choked in surprise. "I thought—I—"

"Yeah. You thought I didn't know I was putting ideas in your head. Look, kid—I didn't quite tell that story to you straight. It was the second trip to the Moon—and *I* was the kid who stowed away on it. But unless you could figure it out for yourself—with a little help—you didn't deserve a chance. How about the clothes?"

"You probably brought some along," Chuck guessed, laughing.

"Smart boy." Jeff pointed to a bag at his side. "But you haven't figured yet what you'd do to get aboard? It isn't a pushover—they have guards around the ship. And if you're found before take-off, they'll practically clap you in irons."

"I know it. But I was figuring that maybe I could slip past the guards."

"Not a chance. There's an electric eye system the guard has to let down—I've been looking it over on the quiet. We'll have to work it out some way, but I'm not sure yet how."

Chuck climbed into the new space suit, while Jeff put on his old one. They started toward the tractor port, and Chuck frowned. He'd expected to travel on foot to the *Eros*. Then he realized Jeff was right; the only thing was to act as if they were on legitimate business.

He put his head against the pilot's.

"How about you, Jeff? Are you sure it won't get you in trouble?"

"Maybe—but I've been in trouble before. I used to be something of a character. I'll make out. And Chuck—"

"Yes?"

"If we see Vance or Steele, forget everything. They'd have to turn you in, since they're officials responsible to the UN. Otherwise, get aboard somehow, and leave the guards up to me. I may be able to swing it."

It didn't sound as easy as Chuck had thought. When they got to the ship, it looked worse. The place was lighted, though not brightly, and the single guard was directly below the air lock.

Chuck swung off the tractor and headed forward, fiddling with the tiny dial on his chest that tuned the radio. He kept calling until the other's voice was suddenly in his ears. "Who is it? Wong?"

"Chuck Svensen. I came to pick up some tools I suddenly remembered I'd left. Any chance of going inside?"

"Oh, Chuck." It was one of the construction crew. The man nodded. "No reason why you can't go up; you know the ship. We're just keeping fools from getting lost inside, if they get curious. What about Foldingchair, though?"

"He's just waiting for me," Chuck answered. "I may be quite a while locating the tools, though."

The guard laughed. "Want a good look around, eh? Okay, I know how you feel. If you're not back when I go off, I'll tell my relief to let you out. The beam's off—go ahead."

Chuck grunted unhappily. He'd been hoping they wouldn't maintain a guard up till the last minute, but the "relief" sounded as if they were taking no chances. But it was too late to back out. He went up the ladder and into the ship. Jeff touched helmets with the guard.

The guard's radio carried the words. "How about letting me in the radar-shack for a smoke, Red? I'll give you a chance afterwards, if you like."

"You've got a bargain, Foldingchair." There was no suspicion in Red's voice. "I've been dying for a smoke. Door's open."

Chuck found his way to the third level of the hydroponics rooms. It was filled with tanks of weedlike plants in chemical-soaked foam-plastic "soil." The low ceiling was blazing with fluorescent lights. Here the carbon dioxide would be released again for re-use. It formed a balance that would make it unnecessary to take along much extra oxygen in high-pressure tanks, and there was no limit to the length of time the air could be used that way.

He moved toward the center of the deck, where equipment for tending the plants was stored. There was an air-cushion there for use under the tanks, if cleaning was needed. He hauled it out, inflated it from a near-by air hose, and spread it out under one of the tanks. There was just enough room for him to slide in, and it formed a fair hiding place.

Jeff's voice reached him again. "Thanks, Red. Kid hasn't come out, eh? I suppose I'll have to wait all night. Why don't you catch a nap, and let me guard? Any reason against it?"

"No—o." Hesitation gave place to relief. "Why not, if you're willing? My relief will be here in a couple hours, but if I can sleep in the shack, I'll be right here for take-off. Thanks, Foldingchair, I'll do you a favor sometime. Wake me up if the kid comes out and you want to leave."

Chuck switched off the radio. Jeff had pulled it off. Now all he had to worry about would be a last-minute search—and Jeff would probably hide the little tractor and claim Chuck had gone home, if anyone asked.

He slipped out of the space suit, hid it under another tank, and relaxed on the cushion. Reaction from the excitement set in, leaving him weak and trembling. But that passed quickly. He was surprised to find himself getting sleepy as the hours passed.

Chapter 5 All Hands to Control

CHUCK's mind was half-asleep, but the shock of the acceleration hit at him before he could begin to sit up. They were using less acceleration here than from an Earth start—the lighter gravity of the moon made less violent beginnings economically sound—but it was still bad.

The cushion had never been designed for such pressure. It sank beneath him, leaving his hips and shoulders against the flat metal floor. He groaned, trying to take up more of the crushing weight on his legs and arms. But it was useless. He had to take it. Then it was too much. Painfully, he rolled onto his side; the effort sent the blood racing to the lower side of his body; then he managed to get over on his stomach. It was almost as bad, but not quite.

The minutes dragged, while he sweated it out. Acceleration seemed to go on endlessly, though it could not have been more than ten minutes.

Suddenly it was over. The recoil of the cushion threw him against the bottom of the tank, bringing a groan from him as his bruised flesh took the force of it.

But he had no time to worry about that. He was on his way to Mars! All he had to do was to remain hidden for a day, and there was nothing that could keep him from making the trip.

He crawled about, using his hands to pull himself along, since there was no weight to anchor him down. In the bag Jeff had packed, he found a plastic container of water and a bar of chocolate. He munched the candy, and drank the water, sucking it through its little nipple. His stomach rebelled at first, refusing to function without gravity to give him weight.

The sound of footsteps sent him scurrying back under the tank before the big figure of Dick Steele came down the handrails from above, hand over hand. The engineer glanced over the huge hydroponics room, and went on down to the lower levels.

Chuck darted out to where he'd left the bag in plain view. He'd been lucky that time, but Steele might see it on the way back. He glanced at the opening for the handrails.

The sound of a gong reached his ears, but he disregarded it. It was too late when he realized what it meant. The rockets suddenly roared behind, slapping him down against the floor. He had barely time to fall limply, and to try to support himself on his hands and bruised knees.

Then it was over. The speed must have been slightly too little, but it had needed only a touch to correct it. Chuck had been braced when it went off. Now

his legs and arms acted as springs, throwing him up
against the ceiling. He grasped for a hold and almost
managed to stop.

But his clawing just missed the mark. He began
sailing along midway between floor and ceiling, heading thirty feet away toward the wall of the ship, traveling as slowly as a falling feather.

He looked down and up, but it would be at least
a minute before he could get his hands on something
to pull him down. He began threshing the air, trying
to swim through it. Each motion of his arms jerked
his whole body in the opposite direction. Swimming
in air was possible, but it was slow and very awkward
business.

"Hey!" He jerked his head around, setting his body
to jerking sharply and saw Dick Steele's head pro-
truding through the central shaft.

The man pulled himself up, braced his legs for a
second, and leaped out. Chuck tried to duck, but the
other had plotted his course accurately. The big arms
suddenly made contact, and the two of them shot together toward the wall. Dick's hand found a post and
pulled them down together.

"Who—Chuck!" The suspicion faded to a grin. "Well,
I'll be switched! Stowaway to Mars! You crazy kid!
Why the dickens couldn't you stay hidden until we'd
gotten farther out?"

His voice became suddenly official. "Charles
Svensen, I arrest you in the name of the United States

for illegal passage on a chartered ship, in violation of UN regulations. You will come with me!"

One big hand held firmly onto Chuck's wrist as he began moving cautiously from tank to tank, using the other hand to keep from sailing out of control. "I'll have to take you to Captain Vance, kid. You know what this means?"

Chuck nodded. It meant that they were still within reach of one of the little rockets and that a radargram back to the Moon would mean he would be picked up within a couple of hours. He cursed himself for his stupidity in not hearing the gong in time, but it was too late to do anything now.

Steele found the handrail and began pulling his way along it. Chuck wriggled in his grasp. "I'll go along, Dick, if you'll let go."

The engineer released him, and he followed Dick up the rail. They went through the living quarters passage to the closed door of the control room where Steele knocked once. He pulled the door open and reached back for Chuck.

Captain Miles Vance sat at the control board staring at the instruments. He was a tall, thin man, and there were touches of gray in his hair in spite of his being barely twenty-seven. His posture showed the Army training that had preceded his work with rockets. Outwardly, he looked like a harsh disciplinarian, but in reality he was one of the most pleasant men to work with Chuck had known. Lew Wong was sitting beside him at the radar, and the black curls of Nat Rothman barely showed up above the third seat as the pilot dug into the readings from his instruments.

Vance looked up as the door opened, a faint smile on his face. His mouth sagged to a round circle of surprise as he saw Chuck, then tightened quickly. "Dick, unless you've got something important, stay out of here until I send for you! I haven't got time for routine details yet. Lew, get back to work! I want reports of the observatory readings. We haven't time to waste listening to congratulations, or chatting with Lunar HQ. Well?"

The last was to Steele. The big man grinned. "Nothing, sir. Sorry." He reached for the door.

Vance's eyes met Chuck's briefly before it closed. There was no sign in them that he had even seen the boy. Then one eyelid came down faintly in a wink, and the captain turned smartly back to his instrument board.

Dick's face broke into an amused grin, and Chuck let out his breath with a whistle. "Do you think . . . ?" he began.

The engineer laughed softly. "I'm not thinking, Chuck. But in a new ship like this, there are lots of things to do. Vance can't be bothered radaring back right now for a ship to come get you. Come on, I'll have to lock you up until he can see you."

Chuck went along, quite content. He dropped into a hammock in the little crew-quarters with a groan of relief. Dick grinned at him and went out, locking the door behind.

Vance would send word back, of course. But it

wouldn't be until they were too far for any ship to
pick up Chuck. The boy went over to the tiny microfilm library fastened to one wall and began catching
up on his reading. He'd missed three issues of *The
Outlander*, and it was time he caught up with that
"Martian bandit" and his exploits; once they were
actually on Mars, all the stories about the planet were
probably going to seem silly. He had to read them
while he could still get a kick out of them.

It was hours later when he heard the door open.
Captain Vance slipped in, pushed himself to one of
the hammocks, and threw a restraining strap over
himself.

"I was just informed you stowed on board," he told
Chuck, his voice severe. "Naturally, I reported it at
once, but we've passed beyond the area where you
could be taken off. So it seems you're to be with us.
Do you know what that means?"

"Yes, sir. It means I'm going to Mars."

"It means you're asking every man here to give up
one-seventh of his supplies and chances for living to
make room for you! You didn't think of that, did you?
You should have thought of it. This ship was meant
for six men, not for seven! It means we have to carry
a man along who has no specific work to do. And it
means that you'll be under arrest until we return to
the Moon, where your case will be up to the Space
Commission. Officially, I can't condone your conduct,
Charles Svensen. But there's nothing I can do about
it. So, as you say, you're going to Mars."

Chuck looked for any sign of joking in the captain's

face, and found none. He thought carefully—and it wasn't a joke. He had decreased the chances for the others. He pulled himself down to a hammock opposite the captain and tried to think of something to say. Nothing seemed adequate.

Suddenly Vance laughed.

"Okay, Chuck, you needed the lecture, and it's true enough too. But who do you think reminded Jeff Foldingchair of the time he'd stowed away? Who do you think got a lunkhead like Red Echols appointed for guard duty? Officially, we resent your stowing away. But the whole crew meant to have you go, and you're here. If we worried that much about giving up a little of our chance for survival, we'd never have volunteered for the trip."

"But the Space Commission—" Chuck began.

Vance laughed again. "Chuck, there probably isn't a man on Earth or the Moon who isn't tickled pink that you're with us—it makes a whale of a good story. As for your arrest, the terms are that you will be confined to this ship until we reach Mars! To pay your passage, you'll help any one of us who needs help. Now come on to dinner."

Chuck was still trying to find some way to thank Vance as they came into the tiny mess hall, off the galley. A general shout went up as he came in. He looked at them, grinning sheepishly. Lew Wong was beaming; the others seemed just as pleased.

Nat Rothman usually carried the worries of the world on his face. The pilot was a medium-built man of dark complexion, with the only mustache in the crew. Tonight, the mustache stretched out over a smile broad enough to show all his teeth, matching the grin of Dick Steele beside him. Even tiny Dr. Paul Sokolsky seemed completely happy. His red hair was a blaze around his head, without weight to hold it in place, and he kept trying to smooth it down. But he was the first to reach Chuck and begin pumping his hand.

Then the voice of Ginger Parsons cut through the greetings.

"Chuck, you're just what I need. Come back here and help feed these space-happy bums!"

Chuck went back into the galley, where the cook and photographer of the expedition was busy. The man's homely Irish face was a study of thought as he fussed over the heaters with the sealed cans of food. "What's a cook for, anyway? If I tried to do any real cooking here, the liquids would jump out of the pans, and the solids would float around, burning us all to death. But you're cook's helper, anyhow. Pass it out."

It was an odd meal. Liquids came in little plastic bags with nipples through which the contents could be sucked. All other food had to be kept in plates with lids on them, and speared quickly, before the cover was snapped down. Since anything not fastened down was sure to be a menace to them all, the tables were metal, with forks and knives magnetized to stay in place. Yet it was the happiest meal Chuck had ever eaten.

Vance stood up, holding onto a brace when he had finished his dinner. "All right, men, this was a celebration. From now on, we begin regular routine—and you'll find it's just that; shipboard life isn't going to be exciting, at best. I've left the ship on automatic controls this time, to prove to you that it can be done.

"You'll need that confidence in the *Eros*. From now on, though, we keep regular watches. I'll take the first from eight to four with Parsons; Nat, you and Wong get the four to midnight; and Dick, Chuck and Doc will hold midnight to eight."

He grinned at Chuck. "Except tonight. I've noticed you limping around, so you'll get Doc to bandage you, and go to bed. Orders."

Chuck had smiled inwardly at the idea of anything being routine on the *Eros,* but the first week taught him the folly of such ideas. The Moon shrunk to a pinprick behind them, and Mars remained only a tiny red dot. The stars were the same ones he had always seen. And outside, the eternal blackness of space gave them no indication that they weren't frozen motionlessly.

The only change came from the occasional drop of liquid that got free somehow and collected into a little round ball in mid-air. Chasing after it and trying to trap it gave some exercise, but it wasn't a very pleasant kind—particularly when the liquid was hot.

Even that came to an end when Vance decided to set the ship to spinning so that they might be able to lead a more normal life. The spinning would throw them out against the hull like a weight whirled on the end of a string. Centrifugal force wasn't the same as gravity, but the feeling would be the same. It would make navigation harder, but there was little need for that until they reached Mars.

Chuck heard the wheels of the gyroscopes start to spin, turning up to three thousand revolutions per minute. Here in space, every motion in one direction by any part of the ship was automatically compensated for by an opposite motion on the rest of the ship—Newton had stated it in his second law of motion: "For every action, there is an equal and opposite reaction." It took 10,000 turns of the little six-pound wheel to turn the 60,000-pound ship once; and the whole ship began spinning, slowly at first, and then faster and faster.

When they seemed to weigh about ten pounds each, Vance let it stay, and set them to moving equipment to use the hull as their floor. The ship had been equipped for that. From then on, cooking went back to normal. In the hub, or central well of the ship, they were still weightless, but elsewhere they could walk if they were careful to take it easy.

Chuck found his niche. Half of his watch was spent in the hydroponic gardens, clipping the plants, tending them, and turning the clippings into a fresh batch of chemicals by means of the little chamber where bacteria reduced it all to liquid form. On board ship, everything could be re-used, over and over again; there was no loss, only change and that could be controlled. In theory they could have gone on forever, provided there was enough energy to maintain the processes.

The rest of his working time was spent in cleaning
and in helping Ginger with the galley work. He was
a combination cook, cleaning boy, and farmer.

Most of the communication was done on Vance's
shift, and he rarely saw the radar set. The few times
when the alarm told of a signal coming through, it
was of a purely technical nature, and not particularly
interesting. Once he talked briefly to his father; he'd
been sure that his family wouldn't mind his running
away, but it was nice to hear it confirmed. They were
all proud of him.

As they drew farther away from the Moon, the radar
took more and more energy to operate, and Vance
discouraged using it. The atomic engine could operate
for years to come, but the generators were subject to
wear; all had been designed to weigh as little as possible, and there were only a minimum of replacements.

Most of the free time was spent in various games
or in reading. Ginger had suggested a rough version of
hockey down in the central shaft, where the absence
of weight made it possible to leap from end to end
if the initial push was judged correctly. It provided
exercise and amusement and soon became a regular
part of their lives.

Finally, there was sleep. By the time Chuck went
to bed, he was usually tired enough to drift off without trouble, and to sleep soundly through a full eight
hours.

He was asleep, three weeks out from the Moon,
when the first trouble came.

The gong suddenly cut through his dreams, wakening him so sharply that he fell from the hammock onto the "deck." Without time to get back, he felt the rocket suddenly go on with the full thrust of the jets. His body slid down the length of the deck to crash into the steel plates. Only the shortness of the blast saved him from injury.

Then a call came from the control room. "All hands to control. Meteorites!"

Chapter 6 Meteorites!

CHUCK found Dick ahead of him and the others at his heels as he plunged into the little control room where Vance and Lew were busy. There was hardly room for all, but they had no time to worry about that sort of inconvenience.

"Chuck, take radar!" Vance began barking out orders to the others, but Chuck didn't hear the words. He was sliding into the seat Lew had given up, and his eyes were tracing the lines that now seemed to dart across the screen. With more credits in radar interpretation than Lew, he was the logical man for the job now.

Nat Rothman stood over him, working a small computing machine, while Vance handled the controls.

Each of the streaks on the screen represented a tiny object ahead—the size was indicated by the brightness. Chuck snapped his eye to the indicator, and saw that it was set to show pea-sized objects as medium brightness. Another screen indicated distance.

"Link 'em," Rothman told him.

He brought both images together, each in a sepa-

rate color, on a third screen, and began setting up
the first to show the probable speed of the meteorites
in relation to the ship. This required compensating
for the spin of the ship.

"There!" He pointed to one that was the size of a
small marble and much too close. Rothman nodded
at Vance, holding up one finger. The ship blasted forward for a tenth of a second. They waited perhaps
another second, but no sound reached them from the
walls.

"Missed," Vance said tersely. "But we can't keep
it up. We . . ."

There was a sound like a rifle bullet hitting a steel
shed, and a harsher sound immediately after it. One,
smaller than a pea, had gotten through to them, drill-
ing through the ship and out again. At speeds measured in miles per second, even the smallest particle
was dangerous. Apparently all these were small—too
small for the Lunar observatory to have seen them—
but there must have been a thousand or more in the
space ahead.

"Patch it," Vance ordered. Steele, Lew, and Sokolsky nodded and were gone. They'd have to find the
first tiny hole and the second larger one, slap plates
over them, and weld them in place before the air
could rush out into space.

The swarm had thinned out for a time. Chuck kept
his eyes on the plate, but there were only a few seconds
of grace before they began to run into more.

"That first one must have been as big as a melon,"
Rothman told Chuck. "The automatic alarm went on

and Lew didn't have time to set things up. We were simply lucky. Or we're in bad luck. There isn't supposed to be one chance in fifty of running into a meteorite between here and Mars. They're mostly spread out pretty thin, and we're a small target for all that space."

Although the meteorites swung about the sun in orbits like the planets, they were comparatively rare. There had been only one case of trouble in all the trips made to the Moon from Earth. But the *Eros* seemed jinxed.

Now they were approaching the other edge of the swarm where they were thicker again. Someday there would be fully automatic machinery that figured their courses automatically and instantly, to drive ships safely out of their paths. But that was still in the future. Everything now depended on the accuracy of Chuck's compensations, and the skill of Rothman in interpreting the little data he could get.

"*Two!*" Chuck called, and Rothman signalled Vance quickly.

This time the *Eros* seemed to go wild as the full power of her jets flashed on, and cut off. But it had not been successful, for however close Rothman's guess had been, placing the ship exactly between both was too much to expect.

Something hit the wall of the ship with a shriek of rock against metal. It flashed by Chuck's nose, not a foot away, already white hot from the friction of its passage. It *splatted* against the control board, hissed, and disappeared, leaving a six-inch hole in the wall opposite the tiny half-inch hole it had made on entering.

Air began sighing out. Chuck snapped up the thin ship's log and slapped it down over the larger hole, where air pressure forced it into tight contact. Vance had already covered the smaller hole with an eraser.

Steele came in with Lew and Sokolsky. All three showed signs of bruises from the slamming around they had taken when the rockets went on, but none seemed to realize it. They slid quickly cut sections of metal under the crude stoppers and began work with a small electric welder. In a few minutes, the holes were sealed.

The last of the streaks had vanished from the screens. Chuck turned the radar back to Lew, and reported the fact to Vance, who nodded slowly.

The captain was staring at the wreck the meteorite had made of part of the control board. He moved to the panel and began testing, while Steele dropped down to study it directly.

"Some of the rocket-firing controls are damaged— you'll have an unsteady blast. And that first meteorite wrecked the gyroscopes. We're in a fine pickle."

"Yeah. We're probably safe enough now, until we reach Mars. But we'll have to do some beautiful repair work if we're going to make a safe landing there. Chuck, you did a good job—finer than could be expected. It's not your fault—or yours either, Nat. We came through better than we had any right to. Now the question is, how much and how soon can we repair things?"

He turned to Steele. The engineer shook his head. "I can get the gyroscopes remounted, but they won't hold as high a speed, and I can't promise how long the bearings will work. Chuck, you helped install this mess—take a look at it."

Chuck bent down to the damaged wiring. It was a complete mess. Everything would have to be torn out and completely redone—enough following diagrams and resoldering to last for months. He reported it, while Vance searched through the papers in one of the wall safes for the diagrams.

"All right," the captain told them finally. "Get busy. We've got a lot of time left, fortunately. But we can't tell when we may need things again. Probably we won't even get another meteorite signal on our screens. But I'm not betting on anything."

All the men on the ship were trained at several things. Vance was a fair substitute for any of the men, as was Steele. Rothman was a fairly skilled geologist, capable of estimating the mineral resources of Mars, as well as being a pilot. Doctor Sokolsky was as much of a biologist as a medical doctor. From working with his father, Chuck had most of his father's skill at engineering. Lew had made a skilled hobby of archæology. And even Ginger Parsons, who claimed only to be the world's best photographer and a fair cook, had a good grounding in science and mechanics.

But this was a job for two men only, since there was room for no more. The control panel work fell to Chuck and Lew automatically; Vance or Rothman would be with them, to operate the ship when needed, but they would have to reconstruct the wiring by themselves.

Chuck went for his space suit, preferring from experience to do his soldering without air around; it didn't make a great deal of difference, except for the more delicate work; but there, even the finest wire could be handled with a hot iron without fear of damage. Lew was awkward at first, but once the air was pumped out of the control room, he soon caught the knack.

It was tricky work. The original wiring had been done in sections, using complicated, specialized tools; the subassemblies had then been welded into place and hooked up. Now they had to begin work directly, trusting to extensions on their tools to get into the cramped space, and trying to organize it so that they would finish each section as they went along.

Twice the first day, Chuck had to pull out most of what had been done, in order to get in with parts that had seemed simple enough in the diagrams, but simply couldn't be inserted as they had planned.

There was wire enough, and most of the parts were in stock in the big supply rooms along the central well. But many of the coils had been left out on the theory that they could be wound when needed; it was a good theory, if only one or two coils had to be made. But coil-winding was slow and tedious work.

There were tables that showed how the coils should be wound. But handwork is never exact. The prepared coils had to be tested on Q-meters and other instruments. Sometimes they were satisfactory. More often, time was spent in adding a few turns, removing turns, or squeezing and pulling the coils into the correct behavior. There Chuck's work with his homemade set proved excellent experience; Lew had worked only with standard parts, and was less able to cut and manipulate parts into operating condition.

One section was finally finished, and Vance tried it out. It worked—but it would have taken long hours of practice to figure out how to compensate for small errors.

"It's wired right—I know it is. And everything in it meets the limits set in the specifications," Chuck told his captain. "It should be working exactly as it did before."

Steele grinned at him. "Chuck, this is just like radar work. You can follow specs and get something that does well enough most of the time. But I saw the men who installed these panels. In the shop, they'd tested right on the button. Here, they drifted off. The installation took a long time—because they had to go over everything and rework it. Those panels interact; one of them throws another just a little off."

Chuck groaned. But the engineer was right. When he tested the whole assembly on his meters, he found that it would take days more to regulate its action to the correct degree of accuracy.

Next time, on later panels, he wouldn't worry so much about exact behavior of the individual parts. He'd have to take care of that after the assembly was fixed, anyway.

More long days went by on the next of the three

panels that had been injured; this was only partially hurt. The third one, which did the final job of taking the forces of all seven rocket tubes, calculating their differences, deciding how much that would tilt the ship, and making automatic corrections, would be the real headache.

They were still working on the second panel, making the final adjustments, when Dick Steele came up to announce that the gyroscopes were re-installed. Chuck took time off to join the others in looking over the repair.

It looked as good as the original. Dick had managed to melt down the broken sapphire bearing and re-shape it. Some of the supports were crudely welded, but that would not interfere with the operation.

"How'll it operate?" Vance asked.

"Better than I hoped. I've had to handwind one of the motors, and rebalance it, but it should be good for longer than we'll need it, coming and going. The only trouble is that you'll have to run them a little more gently—they can't start, stop, and reverse as smoothly. It won't matter—unless you're having trouble holding the ship steady when they should be compensating."

Chuck frowned. He was tired, and the strain of the responsibility on his shoulders was beginning to tell on him. "Does that mean I've got to do perfect work on the control panels?"

"Just about," Steele agreed. "If anything, you'll have to do better than the men who installed the stuff in the first place."

Chuck looked at Lew, who shrugged.

"I'll do the best I can," he promised. "But if I've got to make that good a job of it, you'll have to turn off the master panel and cut off the control motors. I've got to find how much they interact and how they throw things off so that I'll know how much to correct."

Rothman started to protest, the lines of worry deepening on his face. But Steele cut him off. "The boy's right," he told Vance. "It's the only way I can see. Good sound engineering practice."

"But if we run into more meteorites . . ." Rothman pointed out. "We need some control."

The pilot mulled it over while they moved back to the living quarters. Then he shrugged. "Okay, Chuck, I guess Vance and I will have to give in. If you have to do it, you have to do it. Go ahead."

The captain agreed. Power was cut from the panel after Chuck and Lew had worked out a system that would take the smallest amount of time. The control room was already a mess of tools and wires, but Vance and Rothman filed in, somber about having the ship lifeless for even an hour. The pilot dropped into the radar seat and began working it unhappily, while Vance sat watching. He seemed unconcerned, and made no protest as the switches went down. He had inserted a small microphone under his helmet seals, and was relaying information on their progress down to the rest of the nervous crew. Chuck could imagine that his version of it was honest, but that it all sounded much more reassuring than the captain really felt.

They were half-finished with their tests when the

helmet radio snapped with Rothman's voice. "Pips on the radar. Meteorites!"

"How much time?" Vance asked.

"A few minutes."

It was too little; the panel could not be put back into operation in less than half an hour. Chuck moved up to the radar controls, and readjusted them to give more precise information.

"I think we'll miss them all," he decided, but he couldn't feel certain of it. Scanning such tiny particles at any distance beyond a few miles—a fraction of a second away—was difficult at best.

Vance looked, and went back to his seat, seeming unconcerned. "It must be the front of the swarm the observatory first spotted—they had to guess at its size from the few big ones they could photograph. I've been expecting them, but I thought they'd be farther on. Well, we'll soon know."

Chuck again tried to make a compensation for the spin of the ship that would give finer accuracy, but he could do little to improve his first setting. Lew watched for a second, and then turned back to testing the panels they were working on. Chuck offered to help, but Vance motioned him back. "I know enough for this, Chuck. Stick to the screens. At least, you can tell us in time to say a short prayer before we get it, maybe."

The pips on the screen were brighter now. Rothman was busily figuring. The worry was back on his face, but his hands were steady in the gloves he wore—which was more than Chuck could say for his own.

He was honestly afraid, and didn't care who knew
it. Rothman and Vance seemed incapable of feeling
fear.

"We'll miss them, I think," the pilot announced. "It
looks as if we'll just clear them. Another minute will
tell."

Something sang against the hull of the ship as he
finished. Chuck puzzled over that; no sound could
carry without air. Then he realized the crew below
must have tuned in their suit-radios; he was hearing
the sounds they heard.

It was like the splintering of ice in a metal bucket.
Vance grunted. "Turn it up, Ginger," he ordered. An
intake of surprised breath answered, and the sound
increased in volume.

"Just dust—too small to pierce the hull, I guess,"
Vance decided.

It disappeared then. They listened tensely for it,
but there was no return. It might have been the micro-
scopic fragments of some meteorite which had col-
lided with something and was still following the old
orbit. But whatever it was, it was gone.

The pips on the screen brightened still more, but
they were out of the center now. Then they moved
away and left no trail. Rothman leaned back, sighing.
"They passed behind us. If we don't find more of them,
we're okay. What's the range on this screen, Chuck?
About twenty-five hundred miles?"

It was close enough, and Chuck nodded. "Unless
you hit a big one with the beam."

"A couple of minutes of our flight. I'll hold this,

Chuck. Go on back to your work. If I see a pip, I'll yell."

Chuck and Lew worked on, measuring and comparing with the notes on the specifications. It was slow, tedious work. They were on the last few minutes of it when a surprised grunt came from Rothman.

"What's up, Nat?" Vance asked quietly.

"I don't know—I'm getting something like television snow on this thing. I don't know whether I'm seeing meteorites or not."

Chuck looked down at the soldering gun Lew was using, and grinned. He hit it with his foot and saw the switch snap back from where it had stuck. "That cure it?"

Rothman grinned back suddenly, and nodded. "Down with theory, Miles. Give me a kid whose father brought him up on engineering. No meteorites."

"And no more reason to keep this off," Lew reported. "We're finished."

With a relieved sigh, Vance threw the switches back to the fully on position. Now, if they had to, the ship could try dodging the impact of a meteorite again.

Rothman picked up the mass of readings they had, as Chuck stared at them. He reached for his calculator, and motioned the two boys to follow him down to the crew quarters, where they could work more comfortably. This was theoretical material, and here Lew and Rothman together could do more in a few minutes than Chuck would have been able to accomplish in hours.

Chuck realized that the meteorite collision had done some good. They were all beginning to work together as a team, each doing what he could do best without thinking about it; and each now knew what he should leave to someone else.

That was something no theoretical preparation could give them. He began to feel more optimistic than he had for weeks. Somehow, this was a crew that would get itself out of almost any trouble.

He listened to Rothman and Lew working over the books on theory and the results they had obtained. Then he went to his hammock to sleep. It would have seemed like shirking to him before he stowed away; now he knew that it was just good sense to get ready for the work that must come while others who could do this work better carried on.

As he was falling asleep, he suddenly realized that his father had spent years trying to teach him the lesson he had learned here so quickly. He smiled a little—and then scowled to himself in the darkness. It was a fine time to get homesick!

Chapter 7 Mars Ahead

TRAVELING from one planet to another seems like a simple thing, if the ship has power enough to make the trip. In the old days, most people had figured out that all one had to know was where Mars would be, and then head directly for it with all rockets firing. After all, the orbits of the planets were well enough known, and it wouldn't be hard to aim the ship.

Actually, it took a lot of high-powered mathematics to make a good approximation of the course needed. The direct trip could be made, but it would take an incredible amount of force. And even with atomic energy, no rocket would have any excess power.

Goddard figured out the best orbits early in the twentieth century, when the only rockets in existence were mere toys. He discovered that the most economical orbit could be found by drawing the orbit of Earth, 93,000,000 miles from the Sun, and the orbit of Mars, which was 128,000,000 miles from the Sun at its closest point; then, if another circle is drawn which just touches both orbits, it will be the ideal orbit for a rocket flight between the two planets.

Chuck stood in the control room of the *Eros*, resting his hands and studying the chart of their flight with all its markings for days and speeds. Lew was doubled into the ruined control panel, pulling out the mass of bent and fused parts, but the chart was the only thing of any interest to Chuck in the place.

"Stop muttering," Lew told him. "Either read the stuff aloud, or keep quiet. You're reminding me of how much I've forgotten of the schooling I had whenever you mumble a figure and I can't remember it."

Chuck grinned, and began trying to make sense of it over the radio.

It wasn't a simple path. It left Earth on one side of the Sun and went all the way around to the other side before it met the orbit of Mars. Even at the speeds they were traveling, it would take 237 days, from start to finish.

Even then, it was possible only when Earth and Mars were in exactly the right place—which happened over periods that were years apart.

Earth traveled around the Sun at more than eighteen miles a second, and the ship's acceleration had boosted its speed to better than twenty-five miles a second. Now they were fighting against the pull of the Sun, which reached out, trying to drag them inward, forcing them to lose speed until they would arrive at Mars' orbit with only fifteen miles a second left; but that was as it should be, since Mars only traveled in its orbit at that speed. "Simple enough, Lew?"

"If you discount the pull of Mars," Vance commented, as he entered the control room through the lock they had installed. "You make it sound as if we simply drift down and touch without any more work. Don't forget that we'll start falling for Mars as soon as we come near, and we'll have to land with the rockets, unless we want to be smashed flat or burned up in her atmosphere. That's why you'd better get those controls fixed."

Chuck nodded, and took his turn with the wires as Lew came out for a rest. Being a pilot on interplanetary ships began to sound like a worse dose of mathematics than being an engineer.

They were already more than half the way. Now they would begin heading closer and closer to Mars. Already the Sun, as seen through the filters, had shrunk enough to be noticeably smaller.

He pulled a fused box out of the ruins and studied it carefully, comparing it to the diagrams. In the drawings, it was shown as a dotted box around two bars that didn't quite touch—the symbol for a shielded condenser. But this was obviously a lot more complicated than that.

Chuck picked up the small welding torch and began stripping off the twisted, half-melted shielding. Inside was the wreck of a maze of wires, resistors, condensers, and something that might have been crystal rectifiers once. He motioned to Lew. "Make anything of this?"

"Not much. I've been studying that 'condenser,' and wondering how it worked. Doesn't seem to make sense. Give me those specs."

They went over them together, trying to figure it out. Beside the box was a number, as there was beside each part. Lew went back for a book of parts, trying to find it. It wasn't mentioned!

"Nice," he said bitterly. "They must have put a new circuit in just before the specs were printed—so some engineer drew that in, expecting to key it later. And it got passed over. What is it—some pulsing circuit do you think?"

"Must be. Looks as if it takes the pulses from the motors and chops the tops off them—but it must do more than that."

"Put it aside," Chuck suggested. "We can go over it later. You're strong on theory—you'll have to figure what went into it, unless we have a part among the spares that isn't listed in the book."

Vance picked the box up and turned it over. "How important is this?"

Lew shrugged. "I don't know, but I suspect it's the main trick in getting smooth controls. We're playing this by feel, more or less; control is mostly electronic, but it has some twists I don't know about."

Vance put in a call for Steele, but the engineer shook his head as he looked at the box. He picked up the diagrams and began studying them.

There was a cloud on his usually handsome face as he returned the box and drawings. "It's important— I can tell that much. But it's some new development I don't know a thing about. Shall I put the others to work taking inventory?"

Vance nodded tersely, and Steele went out, still scowling.

Inventory of stocks went on while Lew and Chuck

dug farther into the control panel, and began putting it back together, leaving space for the box. Eventually the last piece had been inspected. There was no spare on board.

The time was getting short. They were beginning to draw near to Mars. The planet now ahead of them was just visible on the radar screen, when it was set for the longest range—where it took a planetary mass to affect it.

Chuck worked on testing the panel, while Lew, Rothman, and Steele pored over the diagrams, trying to figure out exactly what the theory behind it was. They had already put in calls to Earth, but the specifications there were obviously different since they failed to show the box at all; the mix-up on the diagrams had obviously been a complete one. Apparently some engineer had come up with a new development, wired it into the circuit, and marked it hastily into the drawings. He'd failed to report his changes, and when the panel passed its tests, it had been installed without any record that it was nonstandard.

Earth was trying to track down the singularly modest inventor. They reported finally that they had found who it was—but the man had been killed in an auto accident the day he finished the panel!

It accounted for the trouble with the drawings, but it didn't help any. Chuck could only suggest that they try to find his working notes and see if they contained any information.

Another week passed before the answer came. The notes had been found and decoded. They were incomplete, and the engineers there had no model to work from, but the general theories had been discovered. They read them off to the *Eros,* spelling each word in triplicate to make sure nothing was lost.

More days went by while Lew, Chuck and Steele pored over the information and the ruined box, redeveloping the dead engineer's theories, and trying to see how to apply them.

Finally they began work on the actual construction, and none of them looked happy. Chuck knew that half of their work was founded on guesses, but he was too exhausted to worry about it. He took the parts that he needed and began assembling them.

"It all depends—" he answered Vance's questions. "There's a tricky coil here, and we can only hope we've figured out how it was wired from what we found of the original. And we don't know the size of the two condensers. We're just making the best guesses we can. If it works at all, we may be able to tune it up properly, and we may not. With enough time, I suppose we could get it working as well as the original—maybe better."

Vance nodded and left them alone. When he came back, the box was installed, and they were frantically adjusting things in it, trying to get a response from it. The needles on their test equipment stood unmoving at zero.

Chuck lay awake a long time that night. He was sure that the box should work. Of course, he was a little weaker on theory than Lew—but he'd been boning up from the technical books in the microfilm library. He was beginning to feel like a machine, with no human emotions left.

It had seemed romantic, back on the Moon, to get into a ship and sail off to Mars, the first human beings to visit another planet. He'd even dreamed about finding life there—maybe even intelligent life. Before he ever thought he had a chance to go on the expedition, he'd become involved with the puzzle of how men could communicate with other intelligent races, and had spent the best part of a summer vacation in studying all that had been written on it.

But that seemed flat now. His muscles ached from straining over the delicate workmanship. His back was weary with tension; and his mind wanted to go around in a continual circle. Sometimes he felt older than any man on the ship—and then he realized that the others were feeling the same.

When he did fall asleep, it was only for an hour. Then some bit of a dream woke him up. Something about his father . . .

With sudden determination, he dressed quickly and went toward the control room. Technically, he had to get permission to use the radar communications set, but all rules had been dropped in the emergency. He snapped it on, coupling his built-in microphone to the set and began calling his father on Moon City.

Some of the tension he felt was in the operator's voice. They must have been as worried as the men on the ship—or perhaps they felt worse, since they were powerless to help. He waited impatiently, until his father's voice answered.

It was a calm, quiet voice. There was the strength and understanding in it he had always found. "Hello, Chuck. What's the trouble, boy?"

Chuck felt like crying as his muscles relaxed slowly. He choked out the facts, stumbling over the words. Then he waited while the message sped to Earth, his father considered, and the answer came back—they were far enough away that even the speed of radar couldn't cover the distance in less than minutes.

"Kid, unless I'm mistaken, you've run into the oldest trouble an engineer has," his father told him. "Take a look to make sure all your power cables are hooked up. I remember I spent two weeks on a job once, and only got the answer when one of the cleaning women pointed out . . ."

But Chuck wasn't listening. He was across the room, staring into the open panel. Lying curled up in one corner, under a maze of wiring, the unattached cable connection stared back at him accusingly!

He couldn't remember signing off or thanking his father, though he must have done it. His next memory was of shaking Captain Vance awake, and yelling for Lew. By then, the whole ship was clustered around him, trying to make sense of his words.

Three hours later the meters indicated that the panel was working according to specifications.

Rothman made a check, and Steele and Vance re-checked. Everything seemed perfect.

"Looks fine," Rothman told them. "You boys have done as well as anyone could—better than anyone except the engineer who figured this out in the first place.

But until we make an actual landing, we can't know if it's perfect. If we're lucky, we'll get down in one piece; when we see how it operates we'll know enough to correct it if it needs it."

He moved cautiously to the controls and fed a short burst of power into the jets. He nodded slowly, the frown still on his face. "If the gyroscopes were trustworthy . . ."

He let it hang there. Then he grinned. "Anyway, let's have a celebration. How about it, Captain?"

Chuck went back to his routine duties, and the regular watches were continued again. Ahead, Mars continued to grow in size, though the spinning of the ship made it impossible to see any detail. The gyroscope wheel was turning over very slowly, cutting the spin down, until they would again be weightless, but Vance was putting no strain on it.

Chuck waited until the ship ceased spinning before he went back to the control room. Here the planet shone ahead, big and red in the near distance. There was air in the control room again, and he heard his breath whistle out sharply.

The markings on the surface stood out plainly. Whether they were "canals" or something else, there was no way of knowing. Still, his eyes proved that the Lunar observatory's photographs had been right. They weren't as straight as the maps had shown them once, but there was nothing like them on either the Moon or Earth.

It could be intelligence, he told himself. Maybe there had been enough atmosphere for intelligence to develop and to start a civilization. Egypt had built pyramids against a gravity two and a half times as great—and China had erected the Great Wall that still stretched across thousands of miles.

What would they find: perhaps there would be no life of any intelligence, or perhaps ruins to show that intelligence had lost its battle with the vanishing air and water. Yet he could hope that somehow some of it had survived.

Steele had come up behind him and was looking out too. The man's big chest lifted in a slow sigh; he shook his head at Chuck. "It's been too long since there was any real atmosphere. Except for a thin, weak dribble of it, Mars couldn't hold her air. She was too small and light," he muttered, as if reading Chuck's mind. "But it's hard to be scientific when you look at that. I keep thinking of strange people coming out to help us. Maybe I should be writing poetry instead of taking up atomic engineering. Well, we'll know all about it tomorrow."

"And if there are people?" Chuck asked.

Steele sighed again. "I don't know. Maybe war. Maybe peace. When I was a kid, I heard tales from my grandmother that didn't make me think much of people—stories she'd heard from the days when my race were slaves. But don't let anybody tell you that men are rotten, boy; they've come a long way. I think it will be up to the Martians. If they're savages, they'll hate us, and fear us, maybe. You can't make friends with people who are afraid of you."

Then he grinned, shaking off his mood. "We're talk-

ing nonsense, Chuck. We'll be lucky if we find anything as advanced as insects down there. Let's get
back to work on the gardens."

Chuck was dreaming of fairylike Martians coming
out to welcome him with wreaths in one hand and
swords in the other when, the next afternoon, the faint
motion of the ship turning over to direct its jets at
Mars awakened him.

He gobbled down a hasty breakfast from a ration
can and plastic bag, and headed toward the control
room. He hesitated outside, and Vance motioned him
in. Only the captain, the pilot and Lew were there.

The screen above the controls showed the surface
rushing up to them, growing as they watched. Rothman was busy with his calculator, and there was a
trace of sweat on his forehead. Vance sat at the controls, as cool as ever, until Rothman finished and
moved for the seat. Then the captain pulled two of the
remaining three seats together and motioned Chuck
into one.

The seats swung back to form horizontal shock
cushions, while the controls slid out until Lew and
Rothman could drop their hands onto them easily.
Vance adjusted a throat microphone that was coupled
into an overhead speaker. "One minute . . . thirty seconds . . . fifteen . . . ten . . . five . . . four . . . three
. . . two . . . BLAST!"

The pressure of acceleration was easier to take in the
carefully built seats. It hit at them, but their eyes remained glued to the screens. Chuck felt a groan slip
from his lips.

The ship wasn't steady. The point of ground at which Rothman was aiming wobbled, and the ship listed from side to side. They could almost feel the control slipping out of the pilot's hands.

Rothman tapped the levers again, harder this time, fighting against the slipping of the ship. Then one of his hands reached against the savage pressure to a switch. "The instrument readings!" he gasped. "When we get down we'll figure out the trouble."

Again he increased the acceleration against the speed, until the meter above registered five and a half gravities. Chuck's eyeballs seemed to burst, and he could barely see the screen. The ship was slowing now.

"Free fall?" Vance's hoarse voice asked from the speaker.

Rothman made no answer, but his fingers suddenly cut off the rocket blast. There was a high, thin whistle from outside to show they were in atmosphere.

Then they were falling free, trying to correct their motion with the tiny steering-vanes on the stubby wings.

Chapter 8 Crackup Landing

R OTHMAN's fingers hovered over the controls; his eyes glued to the screen. His voice came out as a hoarse croak. "Watch out for the bumps!"

Surprisingly, Vance laughed, almost casually. Chuck glanced at Lew and saw the same fear in his eyes that he felt seeping through his own body.

The ship slowly came to true vertical. Rothman hit the buttons again, and another savage thrust drove Chuck back against the cushions. The landscape below began swaying, but Rothman held the buttons down. The surface below had stopped expanding, and Mars was receding.

They had lost all forward speed and were taking off toward space again. Rothman was fighting against the uncertain blast from the slightly unbalanced tubes, and the lack of help from the crippled gyroscopes. He lifted still higher, and cut off the power.

"Number six is the worst," Vance told him. "Can you synchronize number three with it?"

"No—been trying. Might make it with two and five."

The pilot reached for the controls and played with them delicately. Meters danced on the control board. He hit the buttons for the rockets again. It seemed a little smoother this time—but not much.

Chuck was trying to read the indicator needles. This was his fault—if he'd known a little more theory to couple with Lew's there might have been some way to avoid this horrible veering and uncertainty. If they ever got down, he was going to make sure he found out where the trouble lay.

The blast stopped, and Rothman shot his glance back toward Vance. "Want to try it? Maybe I'm getting rattled."

"You're doing okay," Vance told him calmly. "I'm a little rattled too. Even Foldingchair would be sweating at this. All right, take her down again if you can, Nat."

They were falling slowly again, with the very thinnest of air around them—the sound couldn't be heard, but one needle on the panel swung slightly. They must be at the top of the sixty-mile layer of atmosphere that covered Mars.

The ship wobbled, and Rothman had to correct their fall with flicks of the controls that produced only momentary series of bursts from the jets. Then they began picking up downward speed and running into a somewhat more dense atmosphere, where the steering-vanes would help to level it off.

The surface came up closer this time. Rothman waited until they seemed about to crash before he let the rockets blast out. The ship groaned under the force and began to settle to left sharply. He was using more force than was supposed to be safe, but he continued.

Chuck blacked out for a second; the pressure had gone beyond his limits. When he opened his eyes, the ship was shooting upward, the jets were off, and they were being guided by the steering-vanes. Rothman studied the screen until the right moment came and again cut on the rockets, taking them above the sixty-mile limit.

He swung fully around when he cut power. "Miles, I don't have one chance in ten of making it. If you can do any better, take over."

Vance shook his head. "You're the pilot—I can't do it as well as you. Unless you're scared. How about it?"

"Too busy—too many worries. No time to be scared." He was obviously telling the truth.

Vance shrugged. "Then she's your baby. I'd probably go off the deep end if I had her in my hands. Nat, if you have to crash, crash us. It's getting worse. Don't worry about killing us—I'll give you full authorization to do it, if it makes you feel better. But this time get us onto the surface—whole or in pieces."

Chuck grimaced, trying to appreciate the hint of humor in Vance's words. But he wasn't sure it was humor. The captain might mean just what he said—that they had to get down, and might as well get down dead as to keep worrying. Personally, Chuck preferred to go on worrying, but he kept his mouth shut. He knew if he opened it he wouldn't be able to keep from screaming.

Rothman looked down, and back at the screen. "I've got a couple minutes. Toss me a cigarette, somebody."

From one of his pockets, Vance drew out a package and a book of matches. He lighted the smoke, and flipped it toward Rothman. The pilot caught it deftly between thumb and forefinger, and Chuck realized that the trick could never be done by any man who wasn't in complete control of himself.

Rothman drew two deep drags on it, and crushed it out. "Thanks," he told Vance. "Okay, boys, here we go. If anyone has a particular spot where he'd like to be buried, let me know."

There was the sound of air around them again, wailing and shrieking as the ship picked up speed. Chuck tried closing his eyes, but not seeing the screen only made things worse.

The pilot was picking up skill with the steering-vanes now. This time they were coming down as straight as an arrow could fall with the little light-colored spot below centered exactly in the indicator cross lines. As their speed increased, his control of the ship grew firmer, and there was no trace of wobble. If the rockets had been evened, Chuck realized, the man would have made a smoother landing than Jeff Fold-ingchair could ever make. He was *good*.

Rothman cut on the jets carefully, but the wobble began at once; it was getting worse each time just as Vance had said. The sixth jet must be half out of control. The rockets stopped firing after a brief trial, and the ship continued on, smoothing out its course as the vanes took over the steering again.

They were less than ten miles high. Then they were lower. Rothman was calculating under his breath. He held their course down until the ground seemed to surround them. Then his lips tightened. "Here goes!" he shouted.

Again, the jets went on with their absolute maximum, bringing a screech of tortured metal from the ship. Chuck couldn't faint—the tension was too great, even against the impossible pressure. His eyes remained glued to the screen that was now only a hazy blur.

The rockets stuttered and cut on again as Rothman's fingers moved. Something jarred, jerking the ship. One of the leg-fins had hit ground with the rockets still blasting.

Once more, the cut-off came with an almost impossible short burst of sound following it.

But the scene on the screen showed they wouldn't make it. The last burst had just missed, and they were coming down at an angle. They hit, and bounced, to hit again, with shocks like hammers hitting the pit of Chuck's stomach.

For a flickering moment, they teetered on one leg-fin, and almost righted. But luck was against them. The ship tilted back, hesitated, and broke like a tree, to fall on its side.

Something seemed to explode, and Chuck lost consciousness.

Chuck was first conscious of a wet cloth against his forehead. Dick Steele stood over him, watching while

Doc Sokolsky was running gentle hands over his body. "No broken bones. I guess he'll be all right."

Steele's face was covered with blood from an ugly wound across his forehead, but he grinned down at Chuck. "We had it easier farther back—you took the worst up here. Can you move?"

It hurt with every move of a muscle, as Chuck slowly came to his feet, more surprised than pleased. He'd been sure the fall would kill them. Vance and Lew were already standing up, and Rothman came to a minute later.

"All alive, all sound of limb—by some miracle," Sokolsky told them. "The nylon cords on the mattresses took up the shock for us. But the ship isn't in such good condition."

From what he could see, none of them were in good condition, Chuck decided. All were limping, bruised, and obviously hurting with every step. But the pleasure at being alive made up for any other troubles.

"What about the ship?" Vance asked.

Steele answered. "She's pretty badly cracked up. And we're leaking air from a big crack in one of the gardens. It's near the top, hard to get at. The doors won't close, and we've got to fix that at once if we want to live. Chuck, Nat, Miles—you've all had machining experience. Let's get to it."

In such an emergency, the man who knew the most was automatically the boss. The others fell in behind him, traveling along the central well. Evidences of the crash were all over. Part of a supply room had been smashed through, and goods had spilled all over, making it hard to pass.

"Most of the food is okay, I think," Steele told them. "We lost one water tank—unless we can mop it up somehow—and the plants have been ripped loose in a few places. But the motors seem to be sound, and I don't think the rocket tubes were hurt; they're at the tail, where the fall didn't amount to much. I haven't had a chance to look at the fuel, but I haven't noticed any smell of it in the air, and that stuff's strong. Here, you can see the damage."

He pointed upward, along the "deck" of the gardens toward a gaping rent in the metal above them. One seam had sprung open as if it were a ripe melon bursting. There was something over it, though.

"Some of our tent cloth," Steele explained. "I got it up on poles. Stuff holds back most of the air, though it doesn't seal completely."

Vance studied the situation. "Looks as if you've been busy, Dick. Well, we've got plates enough for a temporary patch—we can use thin stuff for that. But how'll we get it up there?"

"Take the sheets outside, and climb up the hull—we can throw a rope over it and pull a couple of ladders up."

Vance nodded, and they turned into the supply room where the heavy sheets were stored. It would probably take about five of the thinner ones to cover the hole properly. Dick picked up two of them, and each of the others grabbed one, together with equipment that might be needed. They headed for the air lock as rapidly as they could.

The inner door came open easily enough—apparently it had withstood the shock. The outer one was more trouble. It refused to open until Dick and Vance combined their strength, using their legs across it and heaving up together. Then it groaned and folded inward slowly.

Underneath it lay reddish sand, packed down firmly into the shape it had taken from the door. Dick groaned.

Chuck reached for a sheet to shove the sand away, and then he realized what had happened. The air lock lay exactly at the bottom of the ship now—the *Eros* had fallen over on its side, putting its whole weight on the door.

"We'll have to dig out—" he began. But Vance cut him off.

"We will—but not right now. We've probably sunk five feet deep in this soft stuff, and we'd have to dig a tunnel up and around. It isn't like honest dirt—look how dry it is—and we'd have to build supports as we went, to keep it from drifting back. Sure, we'll have to dig out—when we've got a couple free days to give to the job. How about the door to the gardens?"

Steele frowned. "All three doors are stuck. If we could shut the outer one only and seal it, we'd still lose most of our air. Anyway, it wouldn't do any good to save ourselves and let the plants die in the stuff Mars calls atmosphere. We have to have them."

They moved back to the gardens, leaving the equipment beside the useless air lock. Vance stopped to close the inner seal since the air would gradually seep out, even through the bone-dry sand.

The tent cloth covering looked thin and transparent over the sprung seam, but it was holding the pressure. It was designed to be used in the Martian deserts, and to keep an atmosphere during twenty-four hours. But it hadn't pressed itself down smoothly—it couldn't, against the uneven tear. And there was a current in the air that showed a continual loss.

Chuck tried to imagine how Dick had managed to get it up, light and manageable as it was. The poles he used had been normal aluminum pipes, hastily tied together to a length of some fifty feet. Probably the man couldn't tell himself how he'd done it; it had been strictly an emergency reaction.

"Have we still got any power?" he asked the engineer. The big man nodded, and Chuck studied the cloth again. "And we have a good supply of paint that's supposed to dry in five minutes. How about pumping it through the hoses and squirting it up?"

"Might work," Vance agreed.

The hose and pump arrived quickly, and the others began dragging up five-gallon cans of paint. Some was trick plastic, and some had an acetone base. "What's the tent cloth made of?" Chuck asked. "Will acetone soften it?"

"I don't know—it may dissolve it completely. But we'll have to try."

They poured the acetone-base lacquer into the pump tank first, and tested the motor. It was working. Dick and Nat took the nozzle of the pump in their hands, aimed it, and nodded. Chuck opened the valve.

A thin stream leaped upward to wash against the metal overhead. The two men directed it carefully against the edge of the tent cloth, until a gray smear appeared. Then Chuck closed the valve. They watched, holding their breaths.

At first, nothing happened. Then the cloth that had been wrinkled at the edges seemed to sag upward, tighter against the metal. It was working—if only it didn't work *too* well, and simply eat a hole through the cloth. Another five minutes passed, and Vance sighed.

"Good idea Chuck. It's working. Stuff dries before it hurts the cloth, and it still softens the cloth enough to let the pressure seal it. Go ahead."

They were almost out of lacquer when they came to the last section of seam. But the cloth behind them was smooth against the metal and the draft was slowing down to a faint whisper of air movement.

They repeated the maneuver with the plastic paint, but it seemed to have no effect on the cloth. It obviously wasn't a solvent for tent cloth. It didn't matter. They were using it to close the pores in the cloth completely, and it was effective for that. Little by little, they sprayed over it until the last bit of clear cloth was covered.

"Should hold for at least a week," Dick approved. Then he glanced down at the plant tanks along the deck. "The paint isn't helping them any."

"They'll grow back—or new ones will replace them.

We're lucky none of the food plants caught the spray." Rothman's voice was approving. "I feel a little better about the mess I got you fellows in now."

Doc Sokolsky finally caught up with Steele long enough to begin dressing the cut. He nodded his agreement with Rothman, but showed little approval.

"Fine. If we have to live here the rest of our lives, I guess it's better to have air. But I'm not sure. Did any of you notice that we've cracked one of the main girders that run down the ship?"

Pain that was almost physical showed in Steele's eyes. "We couldn't—those things carry the entire rocket thrust."

"Sidewise?"

"No-o. No, I suppose they buckle better when they're slapped down on their side. But we can weld and reinforce it somehow."

They turned to Vance, looking for his opinion, as they followed Sokolsky back to where the big girder lay almost in two pieces. But the captain hardly looked at it. He went on toward the control room to come back a moment later with the course chart in his hands.

Everyone was assembled by then. He addressed them all: "We can get off Mars all right. It may take time, but apparently we've got enough supplies—we'll check later—and I haven't seen any damage that can't be fixed; there may be some we don't know of, but let's say there isn't. The real question is, how soon can it all be fixed?"

Steele looked at the others, trying to figure the damage. "Five, six months, Captain."

"Exactly." Vance held out the course toward them. "And we used extra fuel in landing. Once Mars and Earth get out of step, we keep losing ground—we'll need more fuel to return for every month we stay. Either we get off here within ninety days—or we'll have to wait a few years until the two planets decide to get into a favorable position again!"

He passed the course chart to them. "It's up to you. You'd better work a miracle, because nobody ever needed one more."

Chapter 9 A New World

THERE would be no thrill to setting foot on the soil of another planet for the first time, Chuck realized, as he carried the small shovel toward the air lock. The sand in the lock was soil, all right—but this wasn't the classical picture of an explorer claiming new ground.

Lew called after him, and came bringing another shovel. Both boys were solidly muscular, yet not too large to work in the narrow space, and each had independently arrived at the decision that it was time to start while the others were still taking inventory to see how much remained to be done.

The sheets of metal still stood by the lock. Chuck examined the size of the air lock; then they used the doorframe of the inner entrance to bend the sheets into rough shape. They would not stand any great pressure, but they might keep the sand from drifting back down. The U-shape would serve as both roof and walls.

He was drawing heavily on his father's accounts,

which the elder Svensen had heard from the miners, of the hard time the Moon pioneers had suffered.

The sand was finer than any he had ever seen—as fine as the pulverized pumice he had come across in some of the Moon craters. It drifted off his shovel almost like water, as he lifted it into the air lock.

Lew watched him working on it for a while, and then left abruptly. Chuck couldn't blame him; it looked pretty hopeless. But the radar operator was back a few minutes later with a pair of smaller sheets of the thin metal. He caught them in the doorframe as he had seen Chuck do. With considerable prying and worry over the corners, he finally had a bigger scoop shaped so that it would hold water if necessary.

"Earth tools for Mars," he snorted, pointing to the shovels. "The trouble with you, Chuck, is that you're too used to a light gravity—you forget how much of this stuff we can move."

He shoved the big scoop into the soft sand, wiggling it through until it was full. There was no handle, but he lifted it easily enough and carried it back into the empty passageway.

Chuck grinned at him, and began fashioning another scoop of the same sort for himself. It was true—people carried their Earth habits with them and grew too quickly used to the lightness of the Moon and Mars. Once the novelty of being on a light planet wore off, they settled back to the old ways of doing things. They were heavier here than on the Moon, but they still weighed only three-eighths of what they would on Earth.

They began to make progress. Chuck shoved one of the U-shaped supports through the lock, pushing it into the sand as far as it would go. After each scoopful, he shoved it again on the way back for another. It began moving forward, opening a clear space beyond the door. Now the softness of the sand was proving an advantage. It required no reaching to the ceiling, or digging. It drifted down, well within easy reach.

Vance must have heard of their work. He came down, just as they were moving the second U-shaped piece out under the first, and whistled. "Good work! You're making fast progress. Want any relief?"

Their arms were aching, but Chuck knew that there was no other work they could do better. He'd tried the radar and found that it was out of order from the crash, so there was no way to notify Earth.

They angled the second U-piece upward, scraping it along against the side of the ship. Vance returned to the others and Lew went with him to get more metal that they could use for flooring, since they were sinking ankle-deep in the soft sand at each step. With the metal, the tunnel was beginning to take on an air of solidity.

Ginger brought out their food to them, and Vance's suggestion that they'd better take it easy. Later he collected their plates and brought a warning that they'd have to watch not to let the air escape. They'd been too busy to think of that.

"Bring us our suits then, Ginger. And lock both doors to the passage."

"How about the sand there—it's getting out of hand. We could use a man to shove it along as we bring it back," Lew suggested.

Ginger nodded, and they could hear him closing the distant doors. He was back a few minutes later with their suits, a rude form of their scoops, and his camera. His own space suit was on his back.

"Give me a picture for our return, and I'll take care of this myself," he grinned at them.

Now sand began to funnel and blow under the force of the air that was pressing out from the lock through the thin remaining layers of the ashy stuff. Chuck leaned down to draw up the third U-piece, then pressed it forward. It resisted, and gave suddenly, going all the way to the surface. A hole appeared, and sand began running down the tunnel.

It was night outside. Chuck motioned Lew to come up beside him, and they stared out through the hole that was now barely big enough for one man to pass. Chuck opened his radio to the common channel which would also be passed through loud-speakers aboard the ship.

"Captain!" Lew called.

Vance's acknowledgment came at once.

"We're through," Lew announced. "We can see the surface. If you want to send a couple of men to carry all the sand we spilled in the passage back up here, and weld down the passage braces, you'll have a way out."

"Good men. Didn't expect anything so soon. Come

on back, and we'll take over." Vance's approval was too hearty to be anything but surprised relief.

But Chuck had other ideas. "How about letting us go for a little exploration? We've got most of our oxygen, and our lights are fully charged."

"How about weapons?" Sokolsky's voice asked. "No, wait—they're not likely to find anything moving around up there at night—it must be fifty below zero."

"Go ahead, then," Vance agreed. "But not over a mile from the ship—or at least, be sensible. Get back in time to get some sleep for tomorrow."

Tomorrow, Chuck realized, would be a real day. Mars had a day that was only 37 minutes longer than that of Earth; after the fictional nights and noons on the Moon and aboard the *Eros*, it would seem strange to go back to a real night and day. He thanked Vance briefly, and reached for his radio switch.

Steele's voice reached him. "Keep your radio on, kid—we'll be listening. And don't forget the proper ceremony. There's a flag just inside the air lock just for that."

Ginger brought it up to them, his homely face grinning at them through his helmet. "Look pretty when you plant it, boys, because I've got my flashbulbs ready. 'First men to step onto Mars—first alien planet claimed by Earth.' These shots will make heroes out of you guys."

Chuck stuck out his tongue, to express his opinion of being a hero, but he took the flag. Lew had been enlarging the opening, and now they went out to-

gether, onto the cold, chill surface of Earth's neighbor.
Behind them, the flashbulb flashed hotly.

It flashed again as Chuck bent down and inserted
the tiny flag into the ground. "I claim this planet as a
trusteeship of the United States under the laws and
regulations of Earth."

It was a historic moment, and a very solemn ceremony, but he felt a little foolish. It would make more
sense for Vance to claim it. Anyhow, there would be
no one to jump their claim.

Then it hit him, for the first time. This was Mars!
This was the world that held life that never developed
on Earth. He cut on his light suddenly, staring at the
ground around him. It was nothing but arid, barren
sandy waste, useless for anything that he could imagine. Even with the outer temperature far below the
freezing point of water, there was no trace of frost
on the ground.

He started to turn back to the ship in disgust and
fatigue, but Lew had wandered on a few steps farther;
he moved after the other mechanically. If there had
been one little green shoot, it would have been all he
asked. But the Sahara was paradise compared to this.

He tried shouting at Lew, but the air was too thin
to carry more than a high-pitched squeak for a few
feet.

Lew stooped over and held out something. It was
a short object, perhaps two inches long, that looked
like a piece of string. Chuck took it listlessly—and then
straightened. It wasn't mineral, certainly—it could only
be a part of some plant, unless he could believe the

impossibility of its being a piece of paper twine; it
even had the twists that twine had.

Under his helmet light it showed no real details. He
tried to crumble it in his hands, but it was too hard
for that, though it bent a little. Then he noticed that
there were several small hairlike strands sticking out
from it. It must have been the root of a plant once.

He stared about the landscape, while Lew's voice
muttered beside him, high-pitched and far away. It
wasn't until the other tapped his helmet he realized
his radio hadn't been turned on for several minutes,
though he couldn't remember turning it off. He *must*
have been disgusted, if he'd cut himself off without
thinking. His finger quickly flicked the switch in his
glove.

" . . . plant," Lew was saying. "Hey, Chuck. What
do you make of it?"

"It must have been a plant once," Chuck admitted.

There was a sudden shout in their ears, and Sokolsky's voice came rattling in, a torrent of sound. "Wait
boys, wait for me. Don't lose it. It may be the only
evidence of plant life; maybe we're surrounded by
plants, but maybe this was ten million years ago, pre-
served by the dryness. Hang onto it, I'm coming with
you!"

He was coming too—bursting out of the little entrance, his helmet on, but the snaps only half-fastened.
His hands were working on them, while he came
bounding toward the boys in frenzied leaps. "I heard
your description, Lew, it must be a plant, let's see
it. Ah!"

Sokolsky was all biologist now. He crooned over the little rootlet, caressing it in gentle hands. From a string around his neck, he produced one of the little forty-power microscopes and began examining it more closely.

"Well?" Chuck asked, finally.

Sokolsky looked up, and there was reverence on his face. "Cells. Real cells—mummified, of course. But this is what was once alive. Are there more? Where was it?"

Lew pointed ahead a few steps, and Sokolsky bounded forward, his light bobbing on the surface. He didn't stop, but went running on until his figure began to vanish over a rise in the sand and into a hollow beyond.

A sudden shriek sounded in their headphones, followed by silence.

They leaped after him, while all the visions of bug-eyed monsters that were ever imagined on alien planets ran through Chuck's mind. And their first sight of him did nothing to make them feel better. Sokolsky was stretched out flat on the ground, motionless.

Lew yelled at him, and they went rushing forward. But the doctor came to his feet calmly, holding something else out.

It was curled up into a tight ball, with a hard, waxy surface exposed, but beginning to open in the light. And there was no question about it. The bright green color was the familiar hue of plant life.

"There's more—millions more—and dozens of kinds,"

Sokolsky said. His voice sounded ecstatic, but hushed. "We landed in a little barren spot but look . . ."

They followed his gaze, and he hadn't exaggerated. All the vegetation seemed to be balled up into a compact form, probably to avoid any loss of heat during the freezing night. Some of it was largely buried in the sandy ground. But unfamiliar as it was in form, there was at least an acre of ground covered thickly with green objects.

"See," Sokolsky pointed out to them, "the surface is hard, like glass. The plant secretes some kind of wax that keeps it from drying out. And notice how thick the leaves are—they must store water and air—very little as we know it, but a lot for Mars. This will give us a whole new science of life—comparative evolution!"

Chuck found one of the tiny cabbage-like things, and pulled it up. At least forty feet of thin root came up before it finally broke off. He looked at it, and noticed that this one also was opening slowly in the glare of his light. "Do they all move like that, Doc?"

"They have to—they need every bit of light, but they can't stay open when the sun goes down. A lot of Earth plants open and close too—but these have to be better at it. Look at that beautiful root—it probably goes down to some tiny bit of moisture we wouldn't even believe was around!"

Vance's voice cut through their admiration of the tiny plant. "Break it up, boys. It's time to come back now."

"Ten minutes more," Sokolsky asked. "There's one more thing I have to see, Captain!"

"Five, then. No more," Vance agreed. "You can get all the plants you want later."

Sokolsky turned the plant over carefully. "Ten minutes, and I'll find you a Martian city," he suggested quickly.

"Take ten minutes and you'd better produce a city." Vance's voice was sick with irritation, as if one more trouble would snap the tight control and break his mask of agreeableness.

Sokolsky chuckled. "Thanks, Captain."

"He means it," Lew said. "We'd better get back."

The little man shook the red hair inside his helmet, and chuckled again. "I know. And if you'll point your lights over there you'll see the city. You've got ten minutes to look at it—and I've got to find out whether these plants show signs of being male and female."

A joke was a joke, Chuck thought, and started to turn back to the ship. Then his lights swept over the horizon, and his eyes jerked back.

It did look like a city—not a highly advanced one, but like some of the pictures of European ruins he had seen, built of stones that had since crumbled until only bits remained.

Unconsciously, he started forward with Lew at his side. The ruins were probably only natural stones eroded by the winds, but he couldn't stay away.

They were up to it in a few minutes.

It *was* a city of stone, laid out with streets, and

with square, low stone walls outlining what had been houses. Even doors were plain enough—now empty openings. Just inside the doorway of one, a stone bench could be seen—and near it, set into the wall, a seven-pointed star of another color.

Chuck could almost imagine humans sitting on the bench and gazing at the star. But it would have had to be very long ago. Here, with no rainfall, it would surely take at least a million years to weather the stones down to the wrecks these had become.

"Five minutes are up," Vance called.

"Captain, there *is* a city!" Chuck stooped suddenly to pick up a broken piece of what looked like porcelain, glazed, and with a tiny design running in a perfect arc of a circle around its edge. "There *are* ruins here."

"I don't care if you've found native Martians smoking peace pipes. The five minutes are up. If you don't start back, I'm sending Dick out to get you."

Chuck started to throw the shard of porcelain down, but Lew halted him. "Take it easy, Chuck. He's got to get us back, and anything we find is second to that. Let's collect our biologist."

They had no trouble. Sokolsky was already heading back to the ship, smiling to himself. He nodded, holding out three of the tiny cabbage-like plants.

"I've found the answer," he told them. "At least, as much as I can for tonight. There are *three* sexes among the plants. One produces something like pollen, another a different kind of pollen, and the third seems to be equipped to incubate the seed. I don't care if we can't return—just get the radar working so I can call Earth."

Then he sighed, and his face settled into practical lines again. "I hope we don't find infections here that attack the men, though. I'll have to keep a careful check on all the cuts we got from the crash."

"There was a city there," Chuck told him, trying to puzzle out the new man the doctor had become. "Real houses, though they're as old as the hills."

Sokolsky nodded. "I thought so. But I had my luck with the plants, so I left the city for you. There's enough here for all of us. And—you know, boys, it's been two years since I lost my head over anything. I'm glad I did."

Steele was reaching for his helmet as they came through the air lock and his face was shocked and worried. He made no comment, but jerked a thumb and preceded them along the passage toward the mess-hall.

Inside, the others were already assembled with Vance at the head of the table. He looked up, and his hand went down to his lap, to come up with a big .45 automatic.

Chuck laid the shard on the table, pretending not to see the gun. "There were ruins, sir—really. This came from them."

There was a sudden stir among the others as they bent forward, but Vance's free hand picked the shard up and set it aside.

"Very well," he said, in a voice that seemed ready
to break into brittle pieces. "There were ruins. We'll
overlook your disobedience this time. But from now
on, there can be no exception to the rules and orders.
I'm proclaiming absolute, military rule—enforceable
by the death penalty, if needs be."

He sat back, his hand caressing the gun, while
stunned silence fell over the others.

Chapter 10 Marooned on Mars

CHUCK's eyes turned from one to another, looking for some explanation. Their bruised faces were blank, and their scratched and dirt-covered hands remained motionless. As one, they sat waiting for Vance to go on, to laugh at his own joke.

But he didn't laugh. He waited with them, until he was sure that he'd have to speak first. Then his hand reached out slowly for the porcelain shard. "Maybe this is important," he said slowly. "I don't know. Maybe Sokolsky's three-sexed plants are more important than we are. And maybe we're dead, and this is a hell of our own imagining. I don't pretend to know the answers. I'm not pretending to know anything.

"But while you've been learning something, I've been hearing it all. That's why military law is necessary."

He tossed the automatic out onto the middle of the table. "I don't feel like a leader. If someone else is better, select him; or select me, if you must. But whoever leads from now on will have to keep that as a symbol that his word is final. We can't waste time on argument or divided authority. We can't have men staying ten minutes for any reason when they're ordered to return in five. There's the gun—I want everyone who's willing to accept the responsibility to put his hand on it, and we'll take a vote on who it will be."

He waited again, but no hands moved. Finally he reached out and put his own hand on the automatic again; there was no other offer. Vance sighed, and pulled it back to him.

"Very well. Tomorrow we'll go and look at the ruins. We need one day without any duties, even if it makes us feel guilty to shirk what we consider our duties. And from there on, nobody can leave the ship without my permission. You'll remove the radios from your suits when indoors, and you'll call me before doing anything on your own, unless it's work you've been assigned.

"You see—it's worse than we thought. You know about the broken girder, the ripped seam, the damaged goods. Some of you even realize we have the nearly impossible job of getting the ship—more than ten tons of it here—back on its fins. Most of you haven't asked how we'll straighten out the bent frame before we weld it, but it's obvious we'll have to do it by digging sand out from below some parts and jacking up others; probably cutting and rewelding.

"I've been figuring out the time. Four of us will have to do at least one hundred days' work here; part of the work can't be done, except by those four, so the three remaining will have work for perhaps half the time. Rothman, Steele, Chuck and I know how to handle welders—and that means we have full-time jobs. We're figuring on one hundred days' work at twenty hours a day—and we have to be done in less than ninety days.

"Otherwise, we're marooned here—and we can't live until another chance comes for us to go back to Earth. That's all."

He waited for an argument. Chuck looked at the others, and nodded slowly. Silently they agreed, one by one.

Vance smiled suddenly, a weak, dead smile. He broke open the automatic and tossed the empty cartridge clip onto the table. "Good. If you'll accept the idea, you obviously won't need the threat that I used to drive home the seriousness of this. Go to bed, and we'll look at the ruins tomorrow."

He stood up slowly, took three steps forward, and collapsed onto the floor. Sokolsky was at his side at once.

"Strain, fatigue, and loss of blood," the doctor told them. "He didn't tell you he cut an artery in his arm in the landing. He'll be all right with a little rest."

Chuck followed Steele out toward the little bunk room. He was slowly figuring out the fact that Vance had deliberately made one-man rule seem as unpleasant as he could so that they would object to it at once, if they wanted to, and that the captain now felt sure of their obedience. But he hadn't figured some other things out.

"What are our chances, Dick?" he asked. "Honestly."

Dick dropped slowly onto his hammock, and closed his eyes. His voice was almost as tired as that of Vance. "About one in a million, Chuck. Probably less. We're marooned. We might as well face it. But we don't have to take it without fighting back. Go to sleep."

Chuck barely heard the last words, because he was already following them. A whole Martian city, restored to life, wouldn't have changed his actions.

Breakfast was a hodgepodge affair—Ginger was following the orders not to do any work that day without knowing whether he was doing right or wrong, but determined to try. Everyone woke up when they could sleep no longer and stumbled out into the mess hall, where Ginger's sign said: "Help Yourself." Chuck was fairly early. He found a can of protein-vitamin-mineral concentrate and sprinkled it onto some starchy substance in a bowl, figuring it would be a balanced meal. Surprisingly, the combination tasted good, and several others followed his example, though some simply made a quick salad out of vegetables from the gardens.

Vance came tottering in, weak, but obviously back to his normal self. He grinned weakly at them. "Sorry I went West Point drama school on you, boys. Must have been out of my mind. But I still mean it. What's fit to eat in here?"

He followed Chuck's suggestion, washing the food down with a cup of cold instant coffee. "How about the city you found? Who's going along?"

Everybody was going, it seemed. Vance motioned Chuck to lead. They came out of the ship into a late Martian morning. Around them, the sand was still as barren as before, and the little cup into which the ship had settled cut them off from the rest of the planet. The sky above was a deep purple, with two thin wisps of cloud in it.

"We can breathe the air," Steele commented. "That is, we can if we'll compress it enough and moisten it. Right now, it's so dry it'd suck the liquid out of your bodies in a few hours. The ozone layer they talked about seems to be farther up—and that's lucky. We've got oxygen, nitrogen, and pretty much the same stuff as Earth here—only not enough of it."

He turned around, showing the back of his suit. He'd been the last to leave, so no one had noticed it. But there were no tanks. Instead, a set of batteries and a pump was attached. "One for each suit back in the ship. I'll couple them on later."

It was a help. The batteries were lighter and would last longer than the air tanks, and it would save their own oxygen.

They came up to the top of the dune. Chuck caught his breath at the sight below. The plants were all spread out to the sun now, covering almost every square inch. There were no visible flowers, though Sokolsky insisted something similiar was at the end of each leaf. But there was a peculiar beauty to the waxy sheen of the green leaves.

Sokolsky went about, turning up the leaves, which

promptly rolled into tight balls. He came back shaking his head. "Nothing like bugs. I was hoping I'd find some."

"Couldn't this stuff be eaten?" Vance asked.

Sokolsky shook his head. "It's unlikely. I didn't have much time, but the tests I made indicate poisons in it that we aren't used to. Anyhow, the leaves are dryer than facial tissues even if they do look succulent."

Rothman pointed toward the north. "I saw a canal up that way about thirty miles. But there was a lot of desert between here and there. Where's this city, Chuck?"

Seen in the clear light of day, even by the weak and distant sun that could only raise the temperature to about seventy degrees at midday, the city looked less imposing than at night. From a few hundred feet, it seemed nothing but a mass of stone.

Chuck led the way into it. There were perhaps three hundred buildings, all obviously once single-story, and most of them of only one room. The buildings had been made of dressed stone, fitted without cement, but many of them still stood. One, with a sloping stone roof, was almost intact.

The floors were of the greatest interest. Many were inlaid in little colored squares, like a mosaic. Some had geometrical designs, and one showed odd animals, something like a cat-headed buffalo. But toward the center of the city, where the house with the roof stood, they stumbled on the prize treasure of them all.

Something that might have been a tree was worked

into the center. They cleaned some of the dirt and
rubble away to examine it more closely, and Sokolsky
let out a shout.

"Humanoid!"

It was true enough. Standing around the tree were
about a dozen creatures, each vaguely manlike. They
carried themselves upright, with a rounded head, two
arms, and two legs. Sokolsky pointed out that the elbow and knee joints were similiar to those of men—a
remarkable case of parallel evolution. "Probably didn't
look this much like us—all we're seeing is silhouettes
in rather bad art—but they are still more like us than
you'd think. Look—is that a spear?"

They studied it while Ginger took endless pictures,
but couldn't make up their minds. Lew drew out a
knife from his tool pouch and started to dig out some
of the mosaic.

Vance stopped him. "Let it alone. If people have to
vandalize this planet so that future generations who
know more won't have any real evidence, we're not
going to be the ones to start it. We can take back pictures, if we get back—but we won't destroy the evidence."

There were no idols, or evidence of religion, unless
the tree thing was worshiped. It might have been,
though Lew thought that it was probobly another geometrical design, showing some relationship among
peoples or tribes.

Nor was there any evidence of what had happened
to the Martians; they might have vanished, or they
might simply have moved on to other locations. Steele

didn't believe the last. He pointed to the wear on the stones. "It must have been at least ten million years ago when this was built. That's hard stone, and there's only the thin wind and sand to wear it away. They must have died off. Maybe that basin over there held some of the last of their water, and when it went from the atmosphere, they couldn't adapt. 'Gone with the snows of yesteryear' would be more truth than poetry in their case."

Night was falling when they turned back. They knew now as much as they had known before, and no more, except that the original people might have looked vaguely human. But Vance had proved right. The day of rest had been more important than even the pressure of the work.

Ginger broke down enough to tell them where a few precious canned steaks were hidden, and they made a sort of community picnic out of it, broiling them over the little hot plates. The tomatoes and lettuce from the gardens hadn't been seriously hurt, and the salad was officially tossed by Vance.

Rothman alone seemed to have gained no lift from the day. He moved off, still worrying, toward the control room. Apparently the only trace of a sense of humor in his make-up came out only under extreme danger. Chuck followed. His own family had been on his mind more than he'd cared to let the others see, and the radar set might be repaired more easily than much of the rest of the equipment. After all, it wasn't really work; electronics had always been a hobby.

He found Rothman fussing over the communications set. The man jerked up quickly, his dark face flushing faintly. Chuck looked at what he had been doing, and lifted his eyebrows.

"No test instruments?" he asked.

Rothman shrugged. "I worked my way through college—eight years of it—designing these things for a little electronics firm. You get a sixth sense about the inside of them, even if you can't make them sit up and purr. You've lost one of those tubes—someday they'll make them out of nothing but crystals—I'd say; what do you think?"

Chuck wondered how many other talents the man held in check, but he simply nodded. "Maybe. Either that, or there's real trouble. I've been thinking about it. If the spare isn't ruined, we'll soon know."

He located it, and could see no evidence of damage to the case in which it was so carefully packed. At better than $4,000 Earth price for the little thing, it should have been packed well. If it had been solid diamond, it couldn't have been so precious. Yet in his own rig, he was using something that could be picked up on Earth for a couple of dollars; the chief difference lay in the fact that his tube stood some four inches tall, while this took up less than half a cubic inch. Weight-saving cost money.

He plugged it in with the little tool needed to handle it, and cut on power. The indicator light flashed on, and a hum began to come from the small speaker.

"*Eros* calling," he repeated half a dozen times, and switched to receive. It would be several minutes before the message could reach Earth and return, even at the 186,000 miles per second light and radio waves traveled. "Any message to send?"

Rothman nodded. "Just that I'm fine—my wife . . . "

He saw the surprise in Chuck's eyes, and nodded again. "I got married three days before take-off; I didn't lie to the Commission when I said I was single. She insisted on it. I suppose it doesn't matter now who knows."

Vance found them there just as the answering signal came through with its frantic excitement. They'd been given up as dead. Chuck sent quick assurances and a brief report before demanding connection to the Space Commission. Then he turned the instrument over to Vance, who began reeling off facts and figures. They were in luck—there was almost no static.

The others were doing odd jobs; now that some of the shock and fatigue were gone, they couldn't be expected to escape the work completely when they couldn't turn around without seeing something that desperately needed doing. But they were carefully avoiding physical effort as much as possible. Vance had apparently decided to accept the compromise.

The captain came down later, to join them in the mess hall, which was slowly being turned into the chief room. A couple of the inflatable plastic chairs had been set up, and the table had been folded back into the wall. Nothing could make the stern, utilitarian walls of the ship look like home. No room which is designed so that any one of its six walls may be the deck can be given a homey touch. But it was better than the narrow alcoves where their hammocks were set up.

Vance shook his head. "They're trying to figure out the margin I have with the fuel left. It would take us two days to get an approximation, but they'll let us know tonight."

He dropped onto a bench with the fatigue back on his face, though not as badly as the day before. Sokolsky made a gesture toward him and then checked it. Vance would probably worry more in bed than out, his expression said.

But Chuck had gotten fed up with the depression. He'd been hit hard enough himself, and his mood was still one of loose ends and futile gestures. Still, sitting around and watching other men go back to their blues didn't help. He turned toward the hammocks to lie and think by himself, or to sleep if he could.

Suddenly a high, keen wailing sound cut through the room, seeming to come from outside. Chuck felt the hair on the back of his neck bristle. He jumped to the hull, placing his ear against it while the others rushed over to follow his example.

There was nothing for a few minutes. Then it came again—a thin, piping sound that rose to a quavering shriek and died away slowly.

Their faces were gray and taut as they faced each other. "It came from out there," Chuck said, unnecessarily.

The others nodded. Sokolsky laughed nervously. "The wind—there must be a hollow stone. No living lungs could have power enough to make that carry through this atmosphere!"

"There's no wind," Vance told him quietly. "Up in

the control room, I could see the sand out there lying completely still."

The doctor shrugged. "It must be blowing out there, even if it isn't here. It's just the wind."

Nobody could dispute him, though Chuck wondered what force of wind would be needed.

Vance stood up and moved back to the control room. Chuck started toward the hammocks, and then swung after his captain. He arrived just in time to hear the speaker come to life. There was a long preamble about the difficulty of getting exact estimates, but the message finally got down to brass tacks.

"You have fuel enough to reach Earth if you take off in seventy days. Otherwise, you'll have to use too much to reach us, and won't be able to land."

Vance cut the set off sharply and snapped off the lights. He sat staring out toward the desert as Chuck turned and moved softly back toward his hammock.

Seventy days to do work that couldn't be done in a hundred! And if they couldn't do it, they'd have to wait month after month until their supplies ran out before they had another chance.

Suddenly he sat bolt upright, cursing himself. With six mouths to feed, they might make the long wait, if they had to. But his extra burden on their partly ruined supplies would probably weigh the scales against them. Vance's first lecture came back, accusingly. He had no right on Mars. The others had been sent, but he'd stolen his place, and had no rightful claim on the food and water he'd consume.

He got to sleep finally, but it wasn't a restful sleep.

His dreams were worse than his waking thoughts had been.

He saw six graves out in the red Martian desert. There should have been seven, but someone had built a gallows instead, and a straw image of himself was hung there with the accusing details of his murder of the others written on it. As he looked, the straw man came to life and ran after him shrieking in a high wail that his ears couldn't stand.

Chapter 11 *Eyes in the Night*

I T was exactly six o'clock when the sound of a gong woke Chuck. He turned over, growling at the noise, but the gong went on until sleep was impossible. Wearily, he dropped from the hammock to see the rest of the crew doing the same.

Vance's voice was the crack of a drillmaster as it followed the ending of the gong's clatter. "Everybody up and out. We're going to *work!*"

Ginger was reaching for his clothes, mumbling and grumbling, staring through eyes still foggy with sleep for his missing pants. " 'Sa dirty trick. Nobody told me Mars would be like this."

"It'll be worse, Ginger," Vance stated. "From now on, you'll be up half an hour earlier to prepare breakfast for the others. I took care of it this time."

They stumbled into the mess hall, to a heavy breakfast of powdered-egg omelet, bacon, and carefully toasted canned bread. At least Vance didn't mean to starve them to death, as Steele commented.

The captain grinned tightly. "That will come later, if we don't finish in time. Now I expect you to work until you drop dead and then get up and try again. You'll need the food. We've got less than seventy days to get this ship headed back to Moon City—my figures were wrong."

He stared at them, his mouth determined.

"It can't be done," Sokolsky told him. "Men aren't robots—you can't work them twenty-four hours a day."

"Eighteen," Vance stated. "And I wouldn't expect robots to work the way you're going to. We'll let everything go that we can—if it can be fixed after we're space-borne, we'll skip it. We've got to get the *Eros* level and straighten her out. Doc, Lew and Ginger will form the digging crew. I've got a diagram here of where I want the digging to be done. Use what metal you must, but take it easy. The rest of us will start cutting where I've marked the places with chalk. Dick, you can give me a hand for half an hour to make sure I'm right in my figuring; you're a better structural engineer than I am."

He marched them out on the half-hour, assigned them their stations, and came back to pick up one of the welding torches himself. The big acetylene-compressed oxygen rigs were the heaviest tools they carried, and there were four of them. The Space Commission had insisted that four was the minimum number of men needed to repair a major meteor rip in space before they lost more than half their air, and the precaution was useful now.

At noon, when the gong sounded again, Ginger came out with their lunches. Vance set the example by eating his with one hand while he went on cutting through beams with the other. There was another pause for an afternoon snack, and then they worked on until ten in the evening.

"Get to bed," Vance told them. He wiped his hand over his forehead and tried to grin encouragingly. "We've got more done than I expected today—but we'll have to do even more tomorrow."

After three days of that, they were finished with the cutting, and Vance sent the whole crew out to dig, except for Rothman and Steele, who were improvising jacks to lift the section that had sagged.

Chuck's arms lost all feeling after a few hours. He kept telling himself that there was a limit to what the human animal could stand. Then his eyes would go to Vance, who was determined to drive himself hardest of all, and he would realize again that Vance had been right. Robots couldn't do it, but men had to.

He bent forward, trying to step up the count he was using to keep himself going. Beside him, Lew matched his work, scoop for scoop.

That night they finished with the sand, although it took them until two in the morning. Vance pointed out that a single storm would undo half their work unless they did finish, and they went on. Every man grumbled, and most of them protested. But all of them worked.

Chuck unbent his back and headed for the air lock.

Then his glance fell on Vance, conferring with Rothman and Steele, who had been turning the huge jacks
that were raising the middle section. Vance reached
for one of the levers, counting. Chuck took it out of
the captain's hands. The man was swaying as he
moved.

Vance didn't protest. "You're right, kid. I'm being
a fool. If I collapse, I'm a liability on everyone's hands.
Five inches more, Dick, then I'm going to bed."

Dick stared after him, shaking his head. The three
men exchanged brief, weary glances, and bent to the
levers. The ship moved up, a slow fraction of an inch
at a time. And at last that was finished. The *Eros* was
still a wreck, but she rested levelly on the jacks and
the sand, ready for repairs.

Chuck had expected it to take over a week, and it
had been done in four days. But he knew they could
never keep it up. And even if they did, they would
barely make their deadline.

He sighed slowly, dropped down onto the sand, and
fell asleep. Some eddy of semiconsciousness told him
that Dick was picking him up, undressing him, and
putting him to bed. But he didn't have energy enough
to protest.

Vance was up as usual the next morning. "Easier
work today—we're all about shot. We'll take a ten-hour
day, welding the girders back together. The three non-
welders will go back to supplies and separate what's
good from the rest. They can carry the damaged stuff
outside and get rid of it. We don't need extra weight."

He grinned at them, daring them to claim he wasn't

being kind to them. But no one said anything, though there were plenty of unvoiced opinions.

It took them one week to get the *Eros* back in sound condition, as far as her frame was concerned. It was fine progress. But the lifting of the middle section had revealed a series of gashes and separated seams that would require at least five days of welding that had not been on the original schedule. The holes were calked temporarily with the last of the tent cloth and some of the paint, but that wouldn't stay long.

Vance gave no sign that it had upset his plans. He went over the group, one man at a time as they sat at supper, pointing out weaknesses and indicating strengths. He was a living balance sheet, and there could be no complaint of lack of justice in his statements. He went over his own work, as coolly and honestly as that of the others.

Then he put down his pencil. "Vacations are just as important as work. I learned that a long time ago. Chuck, you and Sokolsky have tomorrow off; I'd suggest that you explore a bit—you'll get more rest than just sitting around. Report in the next morning. Next week, I'll pick two others, and they'll be the men who have been the steadiest. But even if I think you've been slacking, you still get a vacation—you just go to the bottom of the list."

For the first time there was a brief mutter of approval, and answering smiles as Vance got up from the table.

He turned back to them. "Thanks for that. I needed a vacation from ugly looks too. Go to bed."

They laughed weakly as he walked out. Steele grinned after him. "You know, I'll bet we work harder next week. But I'm out for that vacation."

They got up in a body and turned toward their hammocks. There was no delay nowadays when it came time to bed down. Only Sokolsky lingered, motioning to Chuck to stay.

"Can you hike?" he asked. "Now, I mean."

Chuck frowned, but nodded. The redhead bobbed up and down in excitement. "I can't, Chuck. But I'm going to, just the same. Vance told me ahead of time, and I've got everything ready—spare batteries, suits, extra food packed into the helmets where we can reach it, and water. I'm going to find out what those canals are once and for all. You can come along or stay. I'm leaving now."

Chuck cursed himself again and started to cut his automatic nod of agreement off. Then he hesitated. If they ever got back to Earth without the answer to the riddle, there'd be no living it down. It was one of the chief reasons for the expedition. He chuckled in spite of himself. He was learning to be more honest, apparently—it was his own chief reason, and it didn't matter about Earth.

"Let's go," he agreed.

Vance was coming down from the control room as they dressed and stopped for a brief wish of good luck. He handed Sokolsky the automatic. "There are shells in it this time. And you might take this compass. It seems to point roughly north."

Then he turned toward his sleeping hammock, and they went down the passage toward the entrance.

The night was typical of Mars—cold air that showed the stars as slightly flickering sparks, low horizon, and a pinprick in the sky that was Phobos, the nearer hunk of rock that served as a moon here. It was only ten miles in diameter, but less than six thousand miles away, and just visible. Deimos hadn't been spotted by any of the men.

Sokolsky headed north, skirting the ruins of the city. He walked briskly, setting a pace that Chuck found hard to match. "Tragedy," he said, pointing toward the ruins. "Stark tragedy. I've come out here nights, sometimes, studying this. There was a rude civilization here once. But no fire and no metals. Did you notice that?"

"No. How do you know?"

"Because I've looked for even one bit of metal. But of course they couldn't have metal without fire—oh, maybe a bit of copper, if they were lucky, but nothing else; and here on Mars that would be hard to find. I've looked for some place where they lighted a fire. Rocks crack under heat. There were no fireplaces, no chimneys. The floors show no fire cracks. I've even tested the glaze on that pottery. It's good clay, but it was sun-baked—must have had some way of concentrating more sunlight on it, but it isn't fired; and the glaze is a kind of lacquer. They didn't have enough air to keep a fire going, even when they built this place. Know why they fell?"

Chuck shook his head, and Sokolsky went on happily. "They didn't have power. The winds here won't do any real work; they had no running streams for water power. No coal—it was never wet enough for a Carboniferous age. No plants big enough to make a fire, even if they could have forced in oxygen enough. Nothing except their muscles. And civilization has to have power—each step up takes more. As soon as they learned about nice things and began to want them, they were licked—they could get them only by laying waste to what should have been saved for the future. And the future starved to death. Tragedy."

It sounded as reasonable as anything Chuck could find to explain the disappearance—if the Martians had disappeared. But there was no way of knowing. He had seen no sign of writing; if they had a literature, it must have been on something that rotted away ages ago.

He wondered if sometime one of the Martians might come across the space ship and marvel at the race who had built this and then vanished, and try to explain it by some fantastic idea.

Again, the thought picked at his mind that if such ever happened, it would be because he had stowed away, robbing six other men of a part of their chances to return. Nobody had mentioned it, and it seemed completely forgotten. But he couldn't hide it from himself. He had no right to the power he was using to compress and moisten the air so that he could breathe it, or to the food he had eaten. He had no right to be on Mars.

The city was behind now, and the soft sand of the desert was making every step an effort. Sokolsky pointed ahead, muttering something. He apparently had some theory as to the distribution of the plants. If so, it was productive of results. They found another strip of plants where the interlacing roots had given the ground some stability, and trudged on. They were making no more than five miles an hour, which was slow here, but Sokolsky seemed content.

"We'll march about halfway there, and then we'll sleep. Ever sleep in a space suit? No? Well, it isn't too bad. I did it on the Moon one night, just to see if it would work. I thought it might be useful. I don't recommend it, but we can sleep anywhere, now that Vance is saving us from ourselves."

He chuckled, to show there was no bitterness in his words. With a chance to explore, Sokolsky seemed incapable of being bitter about anything.

Far away, the hint of a thin, wailing cry cut through the air. Chuck had heard it twice more since the first night, but the hair on his neck still rose at the sound. "Do you still think it's the wind?" he asked.

Sokolsky nodded vigorously. "What else? But not around some natural rock. It's in the city—I've heard it there, closer. But I can't find where. Those ancient people must have made themselves a wind trumpet of some kind that works with very little wind. I'll find it yet. It has to be that."

Chuck wished he could be as certain. It reminded him of the stories Ginger knew of banshees. Nothing good could come of it, he was sure.

Again Sokolsky led across a narrow strip of desert and found another vegetation-covered way for their feet. About half an hour more, according to their progress, and they could sleep. Chuck had begun to wish that he had never come out with the strange, intense little man.

Something rustled across his legs! He jumped, landing with a weak cry, and began inspecting the ground. It was only a long creeper, running for perhaps a hundred feet. Then, as he watched it, it moved forward jerkily.

Chuck swung his light toward the other end. For a brief moment, he seemed to see something scuttle away quickly. He snapped his head around to follow it, but it was gone. The vine lay still now, its balled-up leaves trying to dig back into the sand from which it had been disturbed.

"Did you see anything?" he asked Sokolsky.

The doctor denied it, casually. Chuck wondered. But he was tired and jumpy, and the sound in the distance had upset him again. He had to admit that it could have been his eyes playing tricks on him, and that the creeper had probably been disturbed by his own feet. Yet he seemed to remember standing perfectly still and looking back at the moment he had felt it.

Sokolsky went on a bit farther until he came to another barren patch. There he kicked about in the sand, digging a sort of trough. "This is it, Chuck," he announced. "We'll sleep here until the sun wakens us—I always waken when I see the sunlight. Then we can get a fresh start in the morning."

Chuck studied the sand dubiously. "Suppose a sandstorm comes up and buries us during the night?"

"Piffle, as my old teacher used to say. If it kicks up that much fuss, the sound of the sand hitting our helmets will wake us and we'll find a better place. Anyhow, I haven't seen a good wind on Mars yet—fast, maybe, but not one with any strength to it. I think those precious sandstorms are exaggerated. The wind just picks up the finest dust and blows it along. Somebody on the Moon looks down with a telescope and finds his seeing is cut off—as it is even with a fog. He knows it isn't water, and he thinks of sand in the only way he knows—like the Sahara. So, presto, we have huge sandstorms. Dusty, yes—but buried in sand I won't buy."

When Chuck thought it over, he had to agree with him wholeheartedly. Even against the weak gravity of Mars, it would take a terrific force of wind to give the thin air any real carrying power.

He dropped into the sand beside the doctor, stretching out. The insulation of his suit would protect him from the sub-zero cold easily enough. Anyhow, from what he had seen, the sand was a good insulating blanket. The plants seemed to find it wise to burrow down into it at night.

He turned over on his side as he heard the doctor snap off the radio. It was an act of consideration, since Sokolsky snored rather loudly. Chuck cut his own off.

Something rustled near him. He sat up and the sound went away, but when his helmet touched the sand again, the rustling sound was stronger. It sounded like footsteps—slow, careful steps—in the sand.

He sat up, touching helmets with Sokolsky. "Doc— do you hear anything?"

"Surely—the sand settling under our bodies!"

Chuck remembered beds that had made regular noises until he found the springs jiggled with his breathing. It could be—but he didn't believe it. He lay back, trying to hold his breath.

This time, the sounds were nearer.

He sat up again, and froze. Beyond Sokolsky, perhaps fifty feet away, two huge, luminous circles gleamed at him. This was no illusion. He'd seen cat's eyes in the dark, and this was the same. Cautiously, he touched the doctor and tried to turn the man's head toward the eyes.

There were four of them now, two pairs well apart.

Suddenly Sokolsky sat up with a jerk. The automatic came from his pouch, and the flash of a shot illuminated the night. It was a high, shrill explosion in Chuck's ears.

The eyes vanished, and Sokolsky reached for Chuck, touching helmets. "Quite right, Chuck. They were eyes. I fired into the air of course—it wouldn't do to kill anything as rare as Martian animals must be. If it had been a natural phenomenon, it would have remained; it ran at the sound of the shot, proving it was alive. Maybe you're right about the cries you've been hearing. Hm-m-m. Wonder if it's stalking us, or just curious?"

"What do you intend doing about it?" Chuck asked.

Sokolsky shrugged. "Nothing. We're wearing space suits. I intend to go to sleep."

A moment later, his regular breathing proved that he had lived up to his intentions. Chuck turned around carefully, to face three pairs of shining eyes.

They vanished as he looked, but it didn't make him feel much happier.

Chapter 12 The Mysterious Canals

SOKOLSKY was as good as his word. At the first touch
of the sun, he was up and waking Chuck. Even
before the boy was fully awake, his eyes swung
toward the place where the eyes had seemed to
multiply during the night. But there was nothing there.

Chuck searched the sand for a sign of tracks, but
there was no evidence. If there had been tracks, either
the wind had covered them or they had been carefully destroyed.

Sokolsky was highly amused. "Of course I saw them.
I agree that they were the eyes of some form of life.
Fine. But we are not equipped to track them down,
and all we can do is to report them. Of course, I'd
like to study one—I wonder if they have three sexes,
like the plants—but one must limit oneself to one's
abilities. Anyhow, as I said, they didn't bother us. After
they heard the shot from the automatic . . ."

His hand had gone to the pouch and now it came
away empty. He stared at it in puzzlement, began
searching hastily through his pouch, and then around
the ground where he had slept. There was no sign of
the missing gun.

"But it's impossible. I'm a light sleeper, Chuck. They couldn't have sneaked it out of the pouch without my feeling it. Of course, if I dropped it on the ground . . ." He nodded slowly. "That must be it. I dropped it. But why should an animal want a gun?"

Chuck could offer no help on these animals, or the general psychology of Martian beasts. All he knew was that the gun was obviously missing. On the other hand, the beasts had seemed to be harmless. He'd watched until there were over twenty pairs of eyes; they'd avoided him and disappeared when he looked at them, but by watching from the corner of his eyes, he had seen them increase. A pack of that number could easily have overpowered the two of them.

Yet there was no evidence of any attack. If Sokolsky was as light a sleeper as he claimed, any mouthing of their suits would have wakened him.

Chuck shrugged and tried to forget it. He made an unsavory meal out of the cubed concentrates Sokolsky had put in the little hopper under his chin. At the press of a lever, one cube would be popped up where he could get it. The tube that supplied water was also within reach, but he used that sparingly since it had to moisten the desiccated Martian air as well as supply his thirst. A final check showed him that there was considerable life left in the batteries that powered the air compressor.

Sokolsky was muttering unhappily to himself as they began the journey toward the mysterious canal. It still puzzled him that an animal should steal an automatic.

Then he brightened. "But there is the example of

the magpie. It steals for no good reason. Several other animals do. And there is no way of telling what might smell—if they do smell—good to a Martian animal. Of course."

Chuck smiled. Now that there was an example with which to compare it, Sokolsky was happy again. He was even whistling under his breath as they tramped along. Suddenly Chuck stopped, staring at the ground. "Doc!"

"Eh? Oh, you've found something."

It was part of a footprint—or pawprint. There were four toelike members, the two outer ones smaller than the inner ones; behind that, there was part of the ball or heel of the foot. It looked about half the size of a human footprint.

"At least four-toed—and from the symmetry, it must be four-footed. Wish the back weren't hidden or obliterated." Sokolsky studied it with rapt attention. "Very interesting, though it doesn't really tell us anything. If there were several of them, we could estimate the number of feet, the weight of the animal, and a number of other details. But this is only one, and incomplete. Still, it's interesting to note that nature has evolved the toed foot here on Mars."

There were a number of plant forms that neither had seen before, including one bigger one, something like a head of cauliflower, but with thicker leaves, and about the size of a large cabbage. This one was a dark purple color instead of the usual green. There were several others like it. Sokolsky inspected them carefully, and grinned with satisfaction. "Also three-sexed, though of a greatly different species. It would seemingly be safe to guess that all Martian plant life depends on two pollinators and a single incubator."

Two more hours went by, and Sokolsky began to fret and worry again. He seemed to be able to maintain his calm doctor's rôle as long as he liked, but to go suddenly off on a wild emotional tear as soon as he decided he was a biologist.

"The canals should be here. Rothman said it was about thirty miles north, didn't he?"

Chuck nodded. "We've come somewhere between twenty-five and thirty. We may be short of it by several miles."

Sokolsky agreed, but he didn't look happy. He quickened the pace and went forward at almost a run. Chuck's legs were still sore from the grueling week of work, but he had to stick with the doctor.

They came to a slight rise in the ground and surveyed the country beyond them. There was certainly no sign of a deep trench of any kind, nor of an old river bed, etched out in the billion years ago when Mars might have had water.

But Sokolsky's eyes brightened. "See? There's a darker streak. That must be it."

Again he quickened his pace, and Chuck had to force himself along. But they were less than two miles away, and the space was quickly covered. Sokolsky pointed suddenly, and ran forward while Chuck stared around in an attempt to see what had drawn his attention.

He could see nothing except a great mass of plants

with thick leaves about the size and shape of pumpkin
leaves. But these were waxy and smooth instead of
rough, and they were of such a dark green color that
they almost appeared black in the distance.

"Where's the canal?" Chuck asked.

Sokolsky pointed to the plants. "Right here, Chuck.
The best explanation I could ask to the old mystery,
too. Look at them."

Chuck moved forward until he was standing among
the plants. They were peculiar. Lying along the
ground, and connecting each plant to the next in line
was a grayish rootlike tube. Crosswise, there were
smaller, dark green filaments. But the straightness of
the tubes and the exactitude with which they spaced
themselves out caught Chuck's attention. They looked
like little rows of laundry lines, with the leaves for
laundry. Or perhaps they were like the rows of tele-
graph poles he had once seen.

"Perfectly straight," Sokolsky commented. "Look up
there as far as your eye can see—no, get your head
in line with one of the plants. Now look. What do
you see?"

"A practically perfect row of plants—and I suppose
they're all connected together this way."

"Apparently. Here, cut one of them."

Chuck bent down and pulled his knife from his
pouch. The connecting tube was hard and tough, but
he finally sawed through it. Three drops of thin liquid
oozed out. "One of the first cases of a plant on Mars
which secretes fluid," Sokolsky told Chuck. "Now,
watch what's happening."

The tube had contracted, sending a ripple back from each cut toward the mother stem. It reached, and a second later the broken halves of the tubes fell off. There was a small bud on the northern plant where the tube had been; on the southern one, there was a faint indentation.

"You see," Sokolsky gloated. "They connect. Cut a tube, and it is drained, then discarded. And a new one will grow from this bud to the opposite little socket. Chuck, what did Lowell think the canals were?"

"Just that—canals, built to carry water from the ice-caps at the poles to the rest of the planet when the caps melt in the spring."

"And here you have it—perhaps. See, they run in a straight line—I don't know how wide, but it must be for miles here—as far as we can see. Each of those tubes carries a bit of water one plant farther. It's a regular canal system, Chuck—with a pumping station every two feet, wherever a plant stands. And notice how the foliage differs from other plants here—it would probably photograph enough differently to give just the effect the canals do give."

Chuck stared up the line, and down again. So far as he could see, the plants were in perfectly straight order.

He turned away, disappointed. "I guess I'm a sucker, doctor, but I kind of hoped the canals might turn out to be the work of intelligence, after all."

"And how do you know they're not? Is it impossible for these plants to have intelligence? Could men design a better and more efficient system to distribute the tiny amounts of liquid which accumulate at the poles—a snowcap only an inch or so deep, which only wets the ground when it melts—and yet which these plants may spread to their own kind over the whole planet?" Sokolsky stood admiring them. "A perfect answer to a mystery, and a perfect example of either intelligence or adaptation. I don't know which."

"But it isn't the kind of intelligence I meant, and you know that," Chuck protested.

"You mean animal intelligence, preferably like humans, of course." Sokolsky pondered it, turning to stare across the great "river" of plants, and back to the land around. "I don't know. We may never know the answer to that."

"Why?"

"Well, look. Notice that the land is lower here—we came over a ridge, into a hollow to find these; across there, it seems to be the same way. And it's the same as far as we can see. Maybe these are old river beds—though why they should be as straight as even the most crotchety astronomer admits, I don't know. Maybe they are channels dug up by some race that lived here. Maybe the plants are something they grew to meet the dwindling water supply."

He shook his head. "This is summer on Mars. If these plants produce some fruit, it might not show up for months yet. After all, we're dealing with a year of 687 days. Perhaps they are both food and drink to some race on Mars—or were. But this trip, we can't even be sure of how straight they are. We can say we have solved the secret of the canals—but we haven't. We've left from a thousand to a million questions."

Chuck was still disappointed, though his logic told him that this was a much more satisfactory answer than he had expected.

They stopped to eat and rest. Chuck had expected that Sokolsky would want to follow the canals down as far as they could toward the ship, but the man shook his head. They couldn't find much more than they already knew, and their best chance would be to take a series of pictures as they rocketed up, if they ever did leave.

He leaned back, letting the feeble sun shine on him. "You like mysteries, don't you? Well, consider this. We've found evidence that manlike things lived here once, and maybe a beast like our buffalo—both large animals, highly developed. Even those creatures we saw last night—or whose eyes we saw—were of considerable size and development. But there are no bugs, no small life forms, and so far as I can determine, no lower animal orders at all. Why should this be?"

"Extermination," Chuck guessed. "Hey, wait—that means a high level of intelligence—we haven't exterminated all the pests yet."

"We haven't had the reasons for it that Mars may have had. If they had no chance to live without getting rid of competition, even a fair level of intelligence might do a good job of elimination."

Chuck changed his batteries and stood up. He'd had his share of puzzles and half-answers for the day.

They started back at a leisurely pace, returning over

the same ground that they had covered before. Getting away from the drive and push around the ship had been the best possible answer, Chuck had to admit. He was beginning to feel like himself once more.

"How about sleeping out again?" he suggested.

Sokolsky considered it, and agreed readily. They had enough food concentrate if they were careful, and they might arrive thirsty, but no harm would be done. The batteries were lasting splendidly, and they had spares left. He seemed to feel like Chuck, that the longer they stayed away from Desperation Camp, as he called it, the better off they would be.

They stopped again to rest in the sunlight and to watch the plants moving about, leaves searching for more sunlight, while other leaves tried to climb over them. It had started out as a grueling grind after information but was settling down to a comfortable and pleasant rest. He'd have to recommend it to others.

Finally, Sokolsky stood up. "We'd better get within a mile or so of the camp," he suggested. "Then we'll have time to get in, eat a real breakfast, and still report for work."

It sounded sensible to Chuck. They ambled along, killing time, but doing comparatively little talking. Chuck had expected all naturalists to be busy collectors of specimens, but Sokolsky made it clear that it would be useless now. They couldn't keep the plants properly, and later expeditions with well-equipped laboratories—or actual colonies here—might do a much better job than he ever could. Why start false theories?

He could report on what he saw, with a few specimens and a few pictures. It would be enough.

Chuck wondered about colonies. The plants would probably be the answer to that. Mars had little enough to offer, but Sokolsky had told him that the plants apparently contained all kinds of strange drugs; he'd tried one of them on a cut on his hand to see if it would attack flesh. Instead, the cut was already healed. He was taking specimens of that back. If it proved to be what it seemed, there could soon be a real trade between Earth and Mars.

They crossed their previous camping place and went on. Sokolsky was all for sleeping in the ruins of the old city but Chuck would have none of that. If the noise came from there, he would feel a lot happier on any other spot of ground.

Finally they compromised by finding a little section of sand a mile north of the ruins. The sun was just beginning to sink and the idea of sleep was appealing after the short shift the night before and the long hike. Again Sokolsky turned off his radio and turned over, almost at once drifting off into the deep breathing of sleep. Chuck lay beside him, puzzling over all the doctor had told him. He couldn't make up his mind as to whether Sokolsky had the best mind among them, or whether the man just loved to spout his own theories. But at least he was interesting.

His own body cut off the thoughts by forcing him to sink into heavy sleep beside the doctor.

Then he was suddenly sitting up, with a chill chasing

up and down his back as the final notes of a weird cry rang in his ears. He shuddered and looked around.

There was a circle of shining eyes all about, ringing the two men in completely. Chuck watched them. The eyes disappeared as he looked, but popped up again when he seemed to close his eyes. They could obviously see him easily enough.

He dropped back, planning to wait for a while and surprise them. But something was singing in the darkness—a sound something like the cry of a cricket, but more regular, and somehow softer. He hadn't heard crickets since he was a kid. It sounded good—sounded sleepy. He gave up trying to watch and lay back, letting his eyes fall shut.

In the morning, Sokolsky wakened him, and immediately reached for his pouch. "Didn't you have a knife yesterday, Chuck?"

"Of course. I cut the tube of your plant with it."

"Exactly. And our animal friends must have seen you do it. They came for the knife last night—I figured they would, and sure enough, it's missing."

Chuck searched for it, but without success. It had been in his pouch, and the pouch had been snapped shut. He hadn't opened it since they left the "canal." But the knife was gone.

Clever, those Martians. Too clever.

Chapter 13 On Guard

BREAKFAST was just being served as Sokolsky and Chuck walked into the mess hall. Vance glanced at them and nodded approval. "Good. You both look better too. Tell the next vacationers how you did it so quickly."

Then he swung back to the other men. "I don't care what happened. If one of you lost it—though it seems a little crazy—or even if you found native girls and used it to bribe them into selling you coconuts, tell me what happened to it. A fully equipped welding torch and outfit just doesn't vanish into the air. I'm puzzled."

There was a good deal of heat in his voice. Chuck looked at Sokolsky quickly, and met the other's warning headshake. "What's all this, anyway?" he asked.

Steele answered. "One of the torches is missing—along with a few other tools we've lost here and there, but not really thought much about. But a torch is something that doesn't get lost—and we're sunk without it."

Chuck was amazed at how depressed the group seemed after his hike. He stared from one tired, glum face to another, and back to the desperation on Vance's.

"Okay," the captain said finally. "I know nobody stole it—there'd be no reason. I know the men who have been doing the welding aren't the type to hide it to keep from working—none of you is. And I know it isn't lost. Where does that leave us?"

Rothman shrugged. "Minus one welding torch, two pairs of pliers, one spade, one sheet of aluminum, four cans of corned beef . . . "

The men stood up and began moving wearily out to their work. Vance put his head between his hands, shaking it back and forth. The welding torch was as necessary as he thought, of course. But there was nothing he could do about it.

"We've got an air leak," he announced, as calmly as he could. "Not the ripped seam. That was welded tight yesterday, and the leak is in the wrong section. We spent half the day going around with the smoke candles—and there is hardly a spot on the hull that doesn't have some leak; popped rivets, unwelded welding, and everything else. Our pressure has been dropping. We can make it up with Martian air—but we can't go out into space until it's all sound. We need that torch more than we ever did. But I guess you'll have to take the little electric torch, Chuck, and go around, using it on all the small places we've marked with smoke and chalk."

Sokolsky touched him on the shoulder. "Maybe I know what happened to the torch. We aren't the only life on this planet, Miles. There's a native brand of thief around." He began a carefully toned-down version of the incidents of the gun and knife, stressing his magpie theory. Whatever the creatures saw being used, they wanted. And they were clever.

"Store everything inside, and keep it sealed," he suggested. "You can at least prevent anything else being lost."

Vance shook his head. "Better yet, set a trap. If we can find where they took that torch, we can get it back. I'll bait the trap tonight, and put Ginger to watch over it. It's worth losing a few days' work for."

Chuck went off to his welding, amazed at how thoroughly the crash had opened the ship. There were some of the larger patches that could not be handled with the small electric welder, but he moved along as fast as he could, testing each job with the smoke candle. It would be at least two days of hard work, if he was lucky enough to do it in that time.

By the time night came around, most of the benefits of the hike had worn off. He watched Vance place Ginger outside the ship with a couple of shiny wrenches that had been carefully used during the day, but which weren't essential. The man had slept most of the afternoon, and was now in good shape for the watch.

Vance made his announcement at the table again. "We're laying off most of the welding, except what we have to do. We're going to start unloading the ship— everything that's portable has to come out, and we'll even move the hydroponics and the fuel. With it lightened—and I figure we can get down to around five tons of weight here—we'll undermine the rear, and set winches to work on the rest of it. It's going to be a job getting leverage, but if we sink the rear fairly well, we can make it. The front's a lot lighter, unloaded, than the rear, and that will help."

A groan went up, though not in protest. It was the job they had all dreaded, but one which had to be done. The ship had no chance of taking off and continuing, except with her nose up. But while unloading wouldn't prove too difficult, reloading up through the entrance would be nearly impossible.

Vance's point was that as long as there was any chance of recovering the welder, it was possible. They could strip part of the hull away, and reweld it later. If the welder turned up, they would have saved time by doing work where everyone could be used; if it didn't, there was no loss.

Chuck went to bed without much thought to that. His work with the little torch would go on. After that, he'd probably have to get out and dig with the others, but he'd worry about that when he came to it.

He wondered once how Ginger was doing. There was more envy in his thoughts than anything else. Ginger had the softest job in the place, right now.

In the morning, Ginger reported in disgust that nothing at all had happened. He'd thought something was staring at him once, but it had probably been pure imagination. The tools were still there, untouched. And should he keep guard again that night?

Vance nodded, concerned with other problems. Ginger fished into his pouch and drew out a .45 automatic. "This yours, Captain? I found it fifty feet from me this morning, and figured maybe it slipped out of your pouch last night.

"Thanks. I wondered what happened to it." Vance picked it up without a muscle of his face moving. "Sokolsky, Chuck, stick around."

When they were alone, Sokolsky grinned. "They don't like that brand of monkey wrench, Miles. Or else they've got a cockeyed sense of humor. Bringing back the automatic was a nice touch."

"Sure." Vance opened the gun, and looked at the empty chamber and magazine. "They kept the bullets!"

He turned it over in his hands, and shoved the magazine back in. "Intelligent—but why not keep the gun and use it for a weapon?"

"Intelligent," Sokolsky admitted with a grimace. "The evidence is convincing. And interesting. Suppose you refill that and let me have it. I'd like to stand watch with Ginger tonight—and I'd better if we're going to start moving the contents of the ship out. At that, it might be wiser to move out the fuel and the unused hydroponic tanks first. They're bulky, and shouldn't be of much interest. The rest of the stuff— well, we can worry about that when we see how tonight turns out."

Vance nodded. He lifted his eyebrows when Sokolsky began to put on his space suit to go out to work with the others, and nodded again. Obviously, he'd expected Sokolsky to use the watch as an excuse not to work a full day.

There was more tension that day than ever. The

work was grueling, and difficult. The tanks were small
enough to jockey through the air lock since experience had proved that bigger tanks of the corrosive
fluid failed too often under acceleration. But the inter-
connections and valves made them a mess to handle,
and they insisted on dripping. The outer coating of
the suits gave the men protection enough, but they
had to be careful in handling to see that nothing else
was damaged. In addition, some of the story behind
the missing tools had leaked out somehow, and they
were worried about an inimical native race of some
intelligence.

Chuck came across them as he moved about, finish-
ing the spot welding and repair work, helmets touching. It kept their talk private, where everything on
the radio could be tapped by finding the right setting,
even when supposedly on a private channel.

Sokolsky was looking worried too, for the first time
since he'd started considering the life on the planet.
But he grinned at Chuck, and made light of the sleep
he'd be losing. He seemed capable of almost any degree of endurance, though Chuck would have guessed
that he would be the first man on the expedition to
fold up.

It wasn't a cheerful supper. Somehow, the tanks
had been unloaded onto the sand—both fuel tanks and
unused hydroponic tanks. It represented a grim day's
work, and one that promised even worse efforts when
they had to be put back.

Sokolsky and Ginger slipped out. This time, the bait
was one that had proven itself before—everything ex-

cept the welding torch that had attracted the Martian beasts was spread out in a convenient circle. Ginger and Sokolsky were dug into the sand, beneath the ship, where they could see without being seen.

Nothing came of it. There were no visitors. Sokolsky caught Chuck on the way to bed for a few hours before another day and night's duties. "Eyes all over, Chuck—but nobody was taking the bait. They just sat there, about five hundred feet away."

Chuck nodded and went on down to the tanks, where he would try to find some way of doubling up on the plants to use the smallest number of hydroponic tanks while they were arranging to tilt the ship. He threw out some of the weedy growth that was used only to replenish the air, but could do little else.

With that as finished as it could be, they began digging—the worst work from Chuck's point of view. He tried to envision the big circle they must dig to a depth of better than ten feet as only a group of smaller chunks to be bitten from the soil, but it didn't work. It came out as a group of larger backaches.

The worst part of it all was the general feeling of hopelessness. They were already behind schedule and falling farther behind with each day. Vance couldn't give up, but the others were beginning to do so.

He looked out before turning in to see that the bait was again waiting, with the two men on guard as before, but this time even more carefully hidden. They'd worked it out so that Sokolsky would use the gun, while Ginger would keep his radio on general call, ready to yell at the first sight of the beasts.

It was barely time to retire, though, and Chuck was restless. He snapped down his helmet and went through the air lock, intending to spell Sokolsky for a few hours and let the man get a decent night's sleep.

Then he hesitated. For a moment, he stood in the lock, debating and half-listening for something. Finally, he turned back and climbed into his hammock, falling asleep at once.

Sokolsky and Ginger were not at breakfast as the men came in. Vance cursed, and looked out quickly through one of the windows in the control room. His fingers trembled as he pointed to the place where the "bait" had been left.

Most of it was still there. But the welding torch was gone.

When they got into their suits and outside, they found both Sokolsky and Ginger sleeping soundly, quite unaware of the loss.

Vance's shout over the radio brought them out of it. Ginger woke up groggily, but the doctor sat up promptly, smiling easily. Chuck noticed that a ray of sunlight had been falling directly where his face had been—and remembered Sokolsky's boast of always waking when the sunlight touched him.

Ginger went on yawning, until a startled look came over his face, while Vance hesitated. The doctor, quicker than the cook, swung toward the pile they had used for bait.

He nodded. "Okay, Miles, I've got it coming. I don't have an excuse. You can enforce your military laws about sleeping when on guard duty."

"It's my own fault—I had no right keeping you up without sleep," Vance answered, and his voice was more puzzled than angry. "Ginger, I'll speak to you later. You've had sleep enough and more. Go in and finish breakfast for the men—and then get out there and dig. What happened, Doc?"

Sokolsky shook his head. "Nothing. I was sitting here when I saw Chuck come out. I figured he was going to come over, but he went back in. I'd been a bit groggy before, but that waked me up—or I thought it did. I remember seeing the lock close—and that's all."

"Maybe you noticed Ginger falling asleep, and it hit you—sympathetic reaction after all the sleep you've missed?"

The doctor shook his head unbelievingly. He was obviously completely baffled. Chuck could make no sense of it either. He could understand that the doctor might fall asleep, but the man wasn't the type to keep on sleeping when on duty and with the sun shining fully on him. Something had drugged him—and yet a man couldn't be drugged in an airtight suit . . .

"The blowers!" It seemed too obvious now. "They must be drugging the guard. We get used to thinking that a man in a suit is safe from anything—but we're breathing outside air, compressed, now."

Sokolsky looked sick at the obviousness of it. "I feel logy," he admitted. "Not too bad, but not as sharp as I should feel after a full night's sleep. Well, that's the answer to it, then. Put oxygen tanks back on the guard's suit, and we can go back to normal."

He stood up, stretching. "What's the schedule—more digging?"

Vance nodded, considering it. There was a mixture of doubt and hope on his face. "Yeah, we're still digging. And we might as well get at it. All right, I'll put Dick Steele on the job as guard tonight with oxygen bottles instead of the blowers. But I'm not going to risk another welder. They'll have to take some other bait."

The hole was growing, slowly. The fine sand drifted back almost as fast as they dug it out, and there couldn't be enough shoring provided to do much good. Chuck grimaced at the stuff as he scooped it out. Beside him, Rothman was frowning heavily.

"I quit," the pilot announced suddenly. At Vance's look, he shook his head. "I mean it, Miles. I can't see any sense in digging this out when one good blast from the number one tube would do more than we can do in five days!"

As usual, it was the obvious which had escaped them.

Fifteen minutes later, they stood looking down into a hole that was better than the ten feet in depth Vance had needed. Its sides sloped, as the soft sand ran back into it. But Vance was happy for the first time since they had crashed down on the planet. He admitted that it put him back on schedule, or nearly so.

They took it easy the rest of the day, digging out directly under the tail, where the blast hadn't reached. But by night, they were ready to begin the job of attaching the motor winches and pulling the big ship upright. To Chuck and Sokolsky, he also admitted that it made him a lot happier about wasting Steele's work for a day in sleeping. The big man, knowing all of the story that could be pieced together to warn him, was already out in a new hiding place, watching the bait.

They turned in early, feeling almost pleased to be members of the *Eros* crew again. Even Ginger was forgiven—or made to understand that it was no longer his fault.

It was two o'clock in the morning when they were awakened by the speakers, shouting in Dick Steele's big voice!

The man came storming in a minute later, throwing back his helmet. "I fell asleep—couldn't have been more than ten minutes, but I came to with a sick feeling and saw something streaking away. They've cut through the tent-cloth seal on the underside, and you'd better get down and fix it—you're losing air again."

It wasn't quite true; they hadn't cut through, but had carefully lifted the cloth from the seal around the edges and slipped in—against the air pressure, which must have taken considerable doing. Then they'd left the same way, resealing it somewhat. The loss of air wasn't too bad.

But the loss of the third welding torch was a major catastrophe.

Chapter 14 Welcome Mat

⌈VERYONE knew all the details now, and nobody had
 an explanation. Drugs wouldn't affect a man in a
 completely airtight suit, yet Dick had passed out
 while seemingly wide-awake, and fully aware of
what was going on. To make matters worse, he was
a hypnotic immune. Chuck had thought of the cricket-
like chirping he had heard near the ruins, and had
wondered whether it might not account for his sleeping then, and for his indecision at the air lock when
Sokolsky was on guard.

But a certified hypnotic immune couldn't be hypno-
tized—it was a rare thing, but it had been proved.

Chuck had long since passed out of his depths on
this—but he wasn't alone. There were no theories—
the welder was gone, and that was that. There was
only one left which was capable of mending the big
bottom opening.

That morning they were served minimum rations—
the first sign that Vance was giving up hope, and
expecting to have to stay on until he could find favorable conditions—or until the expedition died.

Nobody commented on it. Chuck got up slowly, leaving half his food behind, and went out, dragging the last welder behind him. Before, the threat to the men's lives had been a questionable one, and the matter of food and air might not have mattered. Now, it was almost certain that they would have to stay on indefinitely.

That meant that he would be shortening their lives by one month for each seven months that passed. It was as simple and direct as that. It wouldn't do any good to fool himself any longer.

He was working at top speed, drawing the edges of the seam together and welding them tight, but his movements were purely mechanical. Yet hardly a minute passed without his looking over his shoulder to make sure some Martian monster wasn't creeping up on him for this last tool.

He stopped while the winches were installed, and moved inside to complete the work. He was still welding when the ship began to slip backward and to tilt upward. The deeper hole dug by the blasts of the rocket had made the job easier in every way. The ship rose to an angle of forty-five degrees, and he could feel the inch-by-inch drag of the winches pulling it back, and farther back.

Then he was finished with the seam, and the ship was again reasonably airtight. There was a month's strengthening and reworking of the big girders needed before she would be space-worthy, but there were no holes left for the Martians.

Carefully, while the ship inched back, he stowed

the welder away. Then he grabbed onto the nearest supports and hung on.

It had reached the critical level, and began swinging. By rights, there should have been winches on both sides to keep it stable—but it had been impossible. The two on the ship were both needed to drag it back at all.

The ship rose to upright position, and swung over beyond that, to rock back again. It bobbed like a child's round-bottomed toy. And finally it found itself a position it liked, almost exactly upright, and came to rest.

Chuck let go the supports and staggered down toward the air lock. His stomach was jumping, but he held it down. He'd been wanting to be a man when his age was holding him back from going; he'd wanted to be a man when the ship came crashing down to its unhappy landing. Now he knew he was a man— and it didn't make him either better or worse— only a little harder and tougher.

He slipped down the ladder to the ground while Vance came running up, protesting that he should have given a warning. He grinned. "It wasn't much more than a little jouncing around—and it was the only way we could get both jobs done when they had to be done."

He turned to look up at the ship, and then down into the hole. The leg-fins weren't too stable, but the ship was standing on her own feet again.

"She'll do—we'll reload her carefully," Vance said. He should have been completely happy, but his face was unreadable. "And I'm wondering when we'll lose the other welder."

"I've got a theory—I think the ruins are the hideout," Chuck told him. "It's the only place they could be. And since it isn't on the surface, they must have some way of getting underground. Does that sound reasonable?"

Vance brightened. "Maybe. What about it, Doc?"

Sokolsky nodded. "They're nocturnal—we only know of their prowling around at night. And that does sound like an underground form of life. Besides, I've heard that screech come from somewhere in the old city."

Steele hefted a piece of pipe in one hand, while Rothman picked up another.

"How about it, Vance? We've got three hours left until night," the engineer asked. "I don't like going around killing off other people—even when they're Martians. But when it comes to kill or die off, I like to live. Anyhow, maybe they won't fight, if we go in with a good frontal attack."

"Somebody has to stay," Vance suggested. "I know they haven't attacked by day—but I don't want them to, either. Two men. That way, in broad daylight, the rest of us can make a search of the city. Chuck, how about you and Dick staying?"

The two men exchanged glances, and Vance nodded. "All right, then it's settled. We'll get what weapons we can, but we'll leave the automatic with you. And if anything turns up, let out a yell—there'll be no talking on the common channel unless it's an emergency."

Any form of action was better than nothing. The men ran off to select their clubs and were back almost at once. Then the five headed toward the city, leaving Dick and Chuck beside the ship. Dick was wearing his oxygen tanks, and Chuck had on the blower device; whatever method was used by the Martians should be hampered by having to deal with both styles of equipment at once.

By day, the sandy waste offered no hiding place, but Dick and Chuck had lost faith in good ideas. By common consent, they dropped down beside the ladder leading up to the rocket, back to back, so that they could cover all approaches.

If anything should be safe, the ship should. Chuck sighed, and leaned back so his helmet touched that of the big engineer.

"If I see even a bit of sand blowing, I'll sing out and you shoot," he planned. "You can do the same."

"Should have kept guard this way long ago," Dick said. "The trouble with us is that we've been so pressed for time that we've wasted most of what we have."

They settled back against each other, leaving just enough room at one side for Chuck's faintly humming blower. There would be no talking—from now on, any sound that went out over the radio would be for warning to those in the ruins. Chuck felt for the switch again to make sure that it was on; it was easy to forget and leave it off once it was cut out for helmet speech.

Nothing moved. The shadow of the ship crept forward as the sun neared the horizon. Once Chuck felt something stir in the sand, and jumped, but it was only Dick shifting position. There was a slight wind and it touched the piled up sand around the rocket ship, sending little rivulets downward.

He shifted slightly, and Dick jumped. They glanced around and grinned at each other, then quickly jerked back to watch ahead for any activity. It was like sitting quietly with a rattlesnake asleep on one's lap.

Sound rattled in their earphones. "There's one! There—he slipped behind that big house!"

A babble of confusion followed. Chuck frowned and waited. Finally Dick's voice came over the phones. "What gives, Miles?"

"Don't know—must be somebody's imagination. Probably one of us saw the shadow of another. Nothing to it. And no sign of any entrance underground. How's it there?"

"Quiet!" Chuck answered, and heard Dick's laugh.

Then it *was* quiet again. They shifted from time to time as the sand slipped from under them, and the space suits proved less comfortable than they might have been. But they were used to that now, and paid no attention to it.

Chuck yawned, and realized that sheer boredom was their biggest danger. He yawned again, and it seemed to make the sound of the little blower a trifle louder; but it was so quiet that his ears had to strain to hear it anyway. Maybe the yawn had cleared his ear passages—inner ear passages. . . . He'd be glad when Vance got back. No wonder the watch got sleepy. He'd be less disgusted with them now . . .

Something in the back of his mind whispered to him. He felt that the suit was getting damp and that the air was impossible to breathe. Must be the blower but it was still running—or was it . . .

He opened his mouth to shout into the radio. But it was too much effort. Too much . . .

Vance's voice was ringing in his ears. He muttered in disgust and some of the blackness went away. He'd been about to do something—but it was hard to remember. Then his head cleared slowly and words began to penetrate.

"Dick! Chuck! Chuck!"

"Yeah." It was hard to get the first word out, but the effort cleared the last of the fog from his mind. "Vance! What happened?"

"That's what I want to know! Wait, we're coming now. Good Lord!"

Chuck swung around slowly, to see Dick sprawled out on the ground beside him. He bent over, shaking the big figure, and the engineer sat up groggily. Then some of the babble in the phones registered, and Chuck swung toward the ship.

It lay on its side again, though this time the entrance was just above the surface. Its fall had left part of the hole, but had filled in under it, where the digging had been necessary. And probably there were new cracks now releasing the air.

Chuck staggered toward it, only half-conscious of what he was doing. But now Vance and the others were coming up over the final rise of the sand and pouring down. They stopped at the side of the ship, staring at it without comprehension.

Finally, Vance turned back, shaking his head. "All right, I guess it wasn't too bad—unless we've cracked the hull some more. And it looks more as if someone lowered it than as if it fell. We can blast and dig out the pit tomorrow. I'd rather have that than lose the last welder."

"Vance!" Rothman's voice jerked them around, and they turned toward him. He was standing over the two winches, pointing at them.

It was a sorry mess. A tank of the rocket fuel had been poured over the winch. The corrosive acid had eaten the cables through, stripped off the cogs of the gears, and generally ruined them completely. They wouldn't be safe to support their own weight now.

The funny thing was that there was no blame on any of the men's faces. They had learned not to blame the failure of any of them, apparently. Chuck stood there, holding back the bitter sobs that wanted to come, and he knew it would have been easier if they had turned on him in a body.

Yeah, he was a man. He knew what it meant. Maybe he did. But he wasn't one when the chips were down. He wanted to go into a corner somewhere and cry.

Then he turned in stunned surprise as the sound of genuine crying hit his ears—a choking, horrible sound, worse than he could remember from childhood. Dick Steele stood over the winches, seeing the final failure of the machinery that had become a part of his life, and knowing that he had been somehow responsible for its destruction. There was nothing weak about that crying—it was a release of rage and futility, but there was no weakness.

Chuck stood frozen for a second longer. Then he turned with unsteady steps toward the fallen rocket ship. They'd never raise it now, he told himself. He'd failed them—it had all been his idea. He'd nailed the lids on their coffins as surely as the inscription in that early dream of his had indicated.

Vance's voice was tired and numb. "Never mind. There's scrap metal, and we've got good welders; if I have to, I can weld new cogs, and cut down pipe to make the new winches. It'll take time, but we can do it. There's still one welding machine on the ship."

Chuck went on into the air lock and down the passage. He'd stored the welder away carefully. He'd done everything carefully. He'd been proving he was a man with the right to work with men.

He opened the cabinet. The welder was gone!

His steps were steadier as he came back down the passage and entered the air lock again. They were frozen as he stepped out onto the surface. He turned his face toward the ruins of the city and began walking, one foot ahead of the other, the other after the one.

Vance came after him, but he went on walking until the man held him back by physical force.

"You don't have a welder, Captain. They got the last one. They came out and let the ship down, burned up the winches, and walked off with the welder."

"I know it." Vance turned him around and led him

back into the group. "Everyone here knew it when you came out. We must be getting psychic about such things—or experienced. We'll weld everything with the electric torch, and we'll dig a deeper hole, deep enough for the *Eros* to slide into it. You'll fix the controls so they balance out—the instrument readings will let you do that—and it won't matter if we do take off at an angle. We'll last until we can make it on our fuel, or we'll take off for Earth and tell them to ship out fuel to us on the little rockets, or we'll crash right into Moon City!"

He stopped for breath and turned to face the rest of them. "You don't believe it—and I don't believe it any more. But we are going to do it because we're men, and there isn't enough trickery on Mars to keep us from doing it!"

Chuck looked from one to another. They *didn't* believe it could be done. Nobody was fooling himself any more. But they were going to go right ahead and try it.

"Let's get in and see what damage was done to the ship," Dick suggested, and his voice was quiet now.

They trooped in, one by one, and began moving up and down, searching with the smoke candles. But there was no sign that there were any new holes. A few tiny leaks along the seams remained, but so slow that they hardly mattered. The *Eros* had been let down gently, with the winches. That was why the cables were still on, instead of having been snapped out of their holds by the force of the shock.

"They took a look at her right-side-up and decided

it didn't look the way it should, so they put her back,"
Ginger said.

"Why?" Rothman asked. "It doesn't make sense. If
they wanted to kill us, they could have waited until
night and let her down with a rush. Why this way?"

Sokolsky shrugged. "It seems fairly obvious. They're
trying to make us stay, not to kill us. This is sort of
a welcome mat. 'Welcome, Earthmen.' As far as they're
concerned, we can stay as long as we like—longer.
They could have killed us all off by now. But they
like us."

"Why?" Rothman repeated.

"Because we have so many nice toys that they want.
We bring them presents—but presents they don't know
how to use. They hang around in the sand—I think I
mean that literally, buried in the sand where we won't
see them. They watch us use the toys. And then, when
they find out what the pretty toys will do, they come
and take them away. Why should they kill us when
they can keep us here to show them the use of more
things? Gentlemen, we're being domesticated!"

Chapter 15 The Martians

T could only be one of two things, Chuck decided. He was sitting in the mess hall with the rest of the crew. But no one was doing much talking. There was no need for early sleep, now; they would have plenty of time in which to repair the ship, if it could be repaired. They might be short on supplies after a while, but there'd be more than time enough.

He turned everything over again, breaking all the elements down and recombining them, but the answer still came out to the two possibilities. It had to be one of them.

He got up, nodding to the others, and moved out toward the air lock where his suit was. The helmet was hanging there, with the little radio inside it. He studied it for a second and then moved on to the tool storage section, now half-bare. All he needed was a small screwdriver, a metal tube, and a new set of oxygen tanks.

When he came back to the suit, he had all of them. The screwdriver helped him to pull the radio set out and toss it aside. The metal pipe slid down one of the little tubes that led to the helmet. And the oxygen tanks replaced the blower he had been using. He studied the outfit for a few minutes. Something was missing.

In the tool supply room he located a fine wire and a small flashlight. Then he began working on the suit again. This time the little plastic tube came out completely, and the wire went down it on the inside. A dab of cement held it in place. He put the plastic tube down, soldered insulated wire to the metal one and led it out to the battery. Soldered connections soon led through the battery to the bulb which fitted snugly inside the helmet, and from the bulb to the wire attached to the plastic tube. Finally, he reinserted the metal into the plastic tube and squeezed it. The little bulb lighted, and he nodded in satisfaction.

He climbed into his suit, snapped the helmet down and picked up the electric torch. The air lock closed behind him.

For a moment, he moved along the hull of the ship and the little torch sparkled in the darkness, spitting against the metal. Again he moved on, apparently paying no attention to anything except the tiny holes he seemed to feel in the hull.

This time he wasn't bored and he knew he wasn't going to become sleepy. It might have been the radio. It didn't seem possible, but there might be some way to heterodyne the signal—shift it to one of a different type that would blank out the brain, which was itself partly electronic in behavior. He couldn't remember a clear case of anyone passing out with the radio off. Sokolsky had slept, but it had been a natural sleep, until he used the radio while waiting; they had gotten him then.

But he didn't think so. That was just an added precaution.

An hour slipped by. He moved closer to the tip of the ship, waiting. He knew it was shock that was holding him up. He knew by now that he was as excited as he had ever been. But while the shock lasted, his feelings were deadened, and he meant to take advantage of it. He was beginning to see that others also had feelings, and that they could be shocked. It didn't matter, if you used whatever you had when it was needed.

The light in his helmet blinked, and then went on steadily. Something was pressing against the tube which carried air up from the tanks to his helmet. So that was the trick. He didn't dare to turn, but he was picturing something that could lie buried in the sand, to slip up and pinch the air hose gently; the men on watch would be bored, tired from overwork, and ready to pass out easily enough; when the air supply dropped down slowly, they'd hardly notice it until they were too far gone to do anything about it; or if it was a blower suit, it wouldn't be hard to slip something slowly over the opening to the blower.

He let the little electric welding torch drop slowly, cutting it off. He shook his head as if feeling drowsy. Then he was down on his face in the sand, and there was a chirping, something like a cricket. Other rustlings reached through his helmet—the creatures were coming out of hiding, chirping to each other.

But he didn't dare look until the rustlings faded a little. Nor could he wait too long. He had the little metal tube to thank for being conscious, but it couldn't help him any longer.

He took a deep breath, raising the oxygen level in his suit a trifle, and jumped to his feet. The big light on his helmet shot out.

The timing had been right. They were ahead of him, just nearing the top of the little dune. He doubled his Earth-muscled, Moon-trained legs under him and set out as hard as his legs would carry him. They were traveling like deer through a forest, but his locomotion was that of a kangaroo on an open plain.

Part of his mind studied them. They were about half the size of a full-grown man, and even more human in their body shape than he had expected, though they were slimmer than any man could ever be. The arms and legs were shaped and jointed like those of a man, and the neck rose from the shoulders in the same way, though it was longer. There were no signs of ears or of long hair on the head. Instead, the whole body was covered with a golden-brown fur that must have been two inches long, judging from the way it fluttered in the thin air. Their lungs were large—but not abnormally so. He watched more carefully, and saw that it was the rate of their breathing that accounted for their ability to survive here. Their chests must be heaving at better than two hundred inflations a minute, as against thirty for a man.

There could no longer be any doubt as to their destination. For the first time, they were caught in the act and they were fleeing for what they hoped was safety: straight toward the old ruins.

He put on a touch more speed which brought him closer to them. Now one threw a wild look back over its shoulder. The face had no nose—apparently the mouth served for everything. The forehead curved back sharply, but not without a good height. And the eyes were as he remembered them—three times the diameter of human eyes, and perfectly round, set as wide apart as the head would allow.

Now the houses were closer and they began spreading out. He kept his attention on the one with the torch. The weight would slow it, and it would certainly want to bring its treasure to the community hive, or however it lived. The creature was squeaking furiously now, as if it felt all rules of life would be violated if such a big, heavy creature could outrun it.

He was within feet of it when it flashed down what had apparently been the main street. He was within inches when it suddenly darted sideways into the house he remembered as having the elaborate mosaic on the floor. He lost it for a second as he overshot the entrance. But it was furiously busy, pressing in some order on the branches of the tree-thing.

The center of the mosaic suddenly lifted, and the creature darted downward.

He leaped forward before the entrance could close and caught it, wrenching upward with all his force. It gave easily; there was no snapping of hinges, as he had thought. He stood holding it, wishing that he'd known enough to leave the radio in his helmet. With that, he could have had the others from the ship here; and a few men should be able to handle hundreds of these delicate creatures, at least when protected by space suits.

He searched for something with which he could leave a sign for anyone who might have missed him in the ship. But even his pouch had been stripped away while he had played unconscious. It was up to him. Or, wait . . .

It seemed like sheer foolishness, but he had to leave some sign. With a quick wrench of his hand, he tore the light from his helmet and threw it down, pointing at the swinging lid that gave entrance. If anyone came from the ship, they'd be sure to see the burning light.

He still had the little bulb inside his helmet where it had served to warn him that the creature had attacked and how the attack was made. It was a new battery, he hoped. At best, the bulb was a dim thing, and there was no reflector for it. It was also located so that too much of its light spread out in the helmet and against his eyes. But it was better than nothing.

The lid dropped down at once, when he let himself over the rim. It banged gently against his helmet, with no particular force, but a quiet insistence. It was thin, but he remembered that it had withstood their walking over it without a trace of weakness.

He hesitated before letting it drop completely. Then he released his grasp, and it settled smoothly into place. When he pushed up against it, it lifted easily.

Apparently he would be able to get out. He hadn't felt at all sure of it.

Now he was in pitch darkness, and he could imagine hundreds of them grouped around him to bring him down. His hand reached awkwardly to the air-tube, and he pinched it gently. The little bulb flashed on. He blinked, trying to keep it from shining directly in his eyes. By sticking his chin out as far as he could, he could just cover it.

It gave a dim light that reached only a few feet clearly, but he could see that he was in a shaft that led downward by means of five-foot steps—probably ideal for such a lithe race on a light world. He dropped over the second one, and took a third, putting him fifteen feet under the ground. There he came to an inclined ramp that led gently downward into greater depths.

He tried to listen for sounds, pressing his helmet against the hard-packed walls, but there was nothing except a confused whisper that could have been anything. The walls looked like clay, though he had seen no clay on Mars, except for the porcelain fragment.

He wasn't worried about trapdoors, or any of the other things that are supposed to be perils to the underground explorer. These creatures obviously had no major enemies, and their economy must have been both too simple and too meager to afford war among themselves. At any rate, they hadn't known he was coming. He walked ahead confidently, keeping his right hand on the wall; most of the time he let the bulb remain off to save the little battery.

He came to a right turn. When he switched the bulb on, he saw that the little tunnel forked, one section turning slightly to the left, the other to the right. He chose the left, since it seemed to remain under the city while the other would have led outside.

Far ahead, light flickered, dimmer than his own. He wouldn't have seen it, if it hadn't been for the fact he was in darkness at the time. It was gone almost at once, but it encouraged him to believe that he was on the right track.

One thing worried him—none of the others that had fled from him had come down the passage. They should have followed the first—or come in behind him.

He glanced at his wrist watch. It would be time for the others to be going to their hammocks. Probably Lew would notice that he was gone. It wouldn't bother him for a while—but Lew had been sleeping poorly lately. In another hour at the most, they'd look for his suit, and realize he was gone.

Would they know where to look? He thought it over, and decided they would have to—he'd talked about the city to them, he'd started to head for it when he found that the welder was missing; and they would realize that he had a legitimate grudge against the Martians he believed to be there. Sokolsky would guess, if none of the others did. The light would be burning long after that—and it wouldn't take them long to break down the entrance, once they knew where to look.

He should have marked his passage. Then he looked down and grinned. He had marked it. The heavy space boots with their cleats were leaving an unmistakable mark that only a blind man could have missed.

He came to another side trail. Now he was less sure about the direction to take. But the light he had seen had been farther ahead, he was sure.

He walked on, counting his steps now, as he tried to estimate where he was. He must be beyond the limits of the ruined city now.

He was also deeper than he had expected to be. The incline was just beginning to level off. But that was all to the good. It meant he was finally coming to the real living quarters of the creatures. It would take caution then—though he doubted that they could hurt him in the suit.

He tried listening again. By now he should have come to something that would show he was on the right track. The creatures must have had trouble with the oxygen tanks for the welding equipment they had stolen. They should have left signs on the floor—but he hadn't seen any.

Again, a light flashed briefly ahead, a bright, hot light. He blinked his eyes, and started forward at a run, but it disappeared almost immediately.

He stumbled over something, and went head-over-heels. For a second, fear clutched at him, until he tried the little light and found that it still worked. He looked back. On the floor lay a can of corned beef, half the paper torn off. It had been partly crushed with something, but no opening had been made.

They must have wondered about that. Or maybe the spies had managed to find out that humans put such things in their mouths. He kicked it aside, surer that he was on the right trail.

But the constant groping through darkness was beginning to get on his nerves. Maybe he should have let the creature get away and gone back to the ship for help. What difference would it have made, as long as he knew how to find the entrance?

He could still go back, of course, but a streak of stubbornness refused to let him, now that he was so near.

Again, light flickered ahead, nearer this time. It was a dull red glow now.

The light was beginning to puzzle him. The air here wasn't really any heavier than that on the surface, and no flame could burn in that low a level of oxygen. The creatures must have some form of chemical light, such as the glow of a firefly—but it would hardly be as bright as the one glimpse had shown.

It came again, as he was thinking of it—the dull, red glow again. And something moved in front of it, apparently carrying whatever gave off the light across an intersecting branch of the tunnel. These underground caverns must widen out eventually, but he wasn't as concerned with that as with finding any of the inhabitants. The light offered a clue there.

He let out a shout, forgetting that it was nearly useless here, and went down the tunnel at a rapid rate, holding the switch closed to keep from stumbling over anything.

There was a startled chirping ahead of him, and one of the ululating shrieks which had given him the whim-whams before. This time he knew what was producing it, and it was bearable.

The light ahead was hard to see with his own bulb glowing, but he saw it as he turned the corner, darting around another corner. He leaped after it this time, disregarding the dangers that might lie on the floor of the tunnel. If he stumbled, he would have to stumble; if he was lucky, he'd find out what was going on.

Now he hit another straight stretch, with the creature closer, and a pale, red radiance barely visible before it. He leaped forward, trying to avoid bumping against the seven-foot ceiling. The creature shrieked briefly, and dropped the source of light. It darted into a dark side trail and seemed to vanish.

Chuck bent over for the light source and halted.

In the light of this small bulb, his own helmet lamp stood out against the blackness of the floor! Its filament was barely glowing now, indicating a short-circuit of some kind. But it was his, without any question. The dent in the top identified it without any possibility of a mistake.

The crew of the *Eros* would have a hard time finding him now!

Chapter 16 Lost in the Caverns

CHUCK stood for a moment, looking at the useless lamp. It left him without any real choice. He would have to turn around and follow his footprints out of the tunnels, go back to the ship, and get help. With enough light and a few extra men, it shouldn't take long to track down the creatures and locate the missing tools.

He switched on his little light again briefly, trying to estimate how much burning time was left in the battery. He could see no evidence to indicate the charge was running down, but he realized that his eyes might have grown accustomed to a change.

Again, it didn't matter too much. He would simply have to flash it on in the briefest possible intervals and make sure his tracks led ahead. Once each fifty steps should be about right. With such intermittent use, even a well-used battery would last for a long time. The way out shouldn't be hard to follow.

Another of the weird cries ran through the tunnel. He wondered if it might be some kind of signal concerning his presence. Well, let them come for him. It would save the trouble of trying to find them later.

The bravado was his first sign of fear. He stopped sharply, and tried to analyze it, but there was no reason behind it. He just knew that he was afraid again—not greatly, but at least unpleasantly.

He looked briefly at the ground for his footprints and headed down the tunnel at a quick trot, counting the steps to fifty. Again he flicked on the light, and checked his course. He was making better speed than he had coming down. The footprints led on plainly, without even a blurriness to indicate that other feet had used the path since he passed.

He had rechecked the path for the twentieth time and made the satisfactory round number of a thousand steps that finally lifted the little cloud of fear. After all, he was a civilized man with a background that had led man across space to another planet. These were only primitives—little humanoids that had gone down the long road from a medium cultural level to a lower one.

Again he reached the figure one thousand. This time he stopped to rest. He should have kept counting his steps on the way down, so that he'd have some way of knowing how far he still had to go.

He looked at his watch; it still pointed to midnight. It had stopped, and there was no way to get inside the plastic cuff of the space suit to wind it again. Look but don't touch! He'd been getting careless about winding it when he went to bed, and now his carelessness was catching up with him.

Abruptly, at the end of his next sprint, his footprints came to a dead end!

He flashed the light longer this time, until something behind him caught his attention. It was the battered can of corned beef. He knew he hadn't turned any corners near here. Yet the trail ended, and the tunnel turned left sharply. The wall looked continuous, yet his prints went up to it and stopped.

He threw his weight against the lying wall; there was no resiliency, and no breaking through. It seemed as solid as the rest of the walls.

He dropped to his hands and knees, trying to find some crack under it with his fingers—still it seemed solid.

The fear came back to him, washing over him more strongly than ever. Now he wanted light—no more than a glimpse of light, but enough to dispel the fears that were rising in him. He pressed the switch tightly, holding it on. The vanishing footprints still stared up at him.

A sudden chirping sound that seemed to come from beyond the wall brought him to his feet. As he watched, the part that had been a wall folded backward, while another panel came out to close off the branch to the left. The chirpings also turned left and faded away.

Ahead of him was the way he must have traveled, since it ran on without curves or branches, as his memory of this section indicated it should. The footprints, however, were missing from it.

He went down it steadily, nevertheless; it was obviously the path he had followed. Soon he was on an upward incline, and he was again sure he had followed the right trail. Soon the steps would appear ahead, and he'd be out of this rat's nest, with its odd revolving doors.

It went on without a break, and he began to worry about the absence of the side trails he had seen before. They were probably closed off by more of those trick doorways.

Then the trail took a sharp downward incline.

Chuck stopped and backtracked, but there was no other way he could have gone. He had come—or had he made a turn somewhere in the early part of his trip? He'd turned right—no, he'd turned left, because that would carry him under the ruins of the city. That meant that on the way out he should have taken a right turn.

He backtracked farther, pounding on the right wall in the hope that some sound difference would show him where the opening was. He moved slowly now, placing the helmet against the wall and tapping. He could find no difference in any section. They were all dull and muffled, as if the sound were reflected from a great thickness of solid earth.

Thirst was bothering him, more so now that he could do nothing about it. He hadn't meant to be away so long, and he had forgotten to fill the tube after he removed the blower unit. He sucked on it without any hope, and was delighted to find that there was still some water left—perhaps half a cup.

Again he began tapping, although he had less faith

in it now. The incline must have been longer than he
had come up, at this location.

Dim light came from behind him—not a brief flicker
this time but a steady glow. He moved toward it,
happy for anything to take him toward something def-
inite. There were probably a hundred exits from this
place, and it might very well be daylight from the
surface, shining down through a crack. It certainly
seemed long enough to be day again.

But the crack was on the wall, not from the ceiling.
He put his eyes to it and looked through. It was barely
wide enough to show him the room beyond.

The dim light was coming from a number of sources.
It wasn't fire, of course, but appeared to be something
painted onto the walls which made them glow. Dim as
it was, he could still see the details with fair clarity.

The first thing that caught his attention were two
of the missing welders. About twenty of the furry
creatures were grouped around them seemingly argu-
ing vehemently about something, since their chirping
was coming at a rapid rate. Another was making
motions with the torch of one of the machines, apparently trying to show how the Earthmen used it.

One, who somehow gave the impression of age,
though there was no change in the color of his coat,
was beating on the ground and clicking his sharp teeth
together. It might have been either agreement or con-
tradiction.

It was the one in the center of the group that interested Chuck the most. That creature was gesturing
upward, and toward the welders. He made another

gesture which was too complicated for any good interpretation; it seemed to indicate that he was searching rapidly.

The old one clicked his teeth together, beat on the ground, and stood up. It seemed to break up the meeting, and they all began separating. One of them moved to the walls and did something to the glowing sections; the glow faded, and the room was in darkness.

Chuck tensed. Before the final glow died, he had seen the creature who had been doing all the gesturing heading straight toward him. Now he waited, moving cautiously back toward the long tunnel, where he couldn't be caught in any of their doors. He pressed his helmet against the wall. There was a stirring sound, and a soft patter that could only be footsteps.

The creature moved directly past him, making little chirping sounds to itself. Chuck began to bless his good fortune as he dropped behind, trying to be silent while he stayed within range of the chirping. He could only interpret the gestures as an offer to go up to the surface and bring back more of the things which had suddenly turned up within easy reach.

When a man doesn't know his way around, it's better to follow someone who does, Chuck decided. He strained his ears, trying to be sure that the chirper wouldn't be able to turn down some other passage and throw him off the trail.

The creature moved ahead steadily though, at an easy pace. Chuck began to expect daylight at any moment. Presently there was a growing touch of light ahead, but it didn't look like daylight.

It wasn't. The creature suddenly appeared against a rectangular opening of the light which swung shut behind him. Another of the cracks, air vents, perhaps, lay near the doorway.

Again, there were two of the welders in the large room, but this was an entirely different scene. There was no idle chirping and beating on the floor here. About twenty of the creatures were busy at various duties—most of them meaningless—near the center of the cavern. Over in the far corner, a compact little group stood around one of the older ones who was scratching on the floor. There was another watching intently, and it was obvious that the older one was trying to draw something and having a hard time getting his meaning across.

Other treasures from the ship stood about the room, along with some strange structures which were of native make. It seemed to be some sort of workshop.

Chuck kept the chirping creature he had followed carefully within his view, even while he watched the others. It might be only a stop before he went on about the errand he had seemed to be bound on. Chuck couldn't do any better at this stage. He watched as the creature moved about the room until it came to a blower unit hanging on the wall, and began preening itself.

There had been no missing blowers when Chuck had left the ship! That was a recent addition to their collection and hardly in keeping with their usual policy. It touched on unpleasant subjects—the suit he was wearing was now equipped only with tanks of oxygen, which wouldn't last as long as one set of batteries for a blower. He must be running low!

The chirper was still preening in front of the blower, but now it began to settle down on its haunches, leaning back against the wall. The huge eyes closed, as if it were sleeping.

It hadn't been planning a trip up—it had been bragging about one already made. Chuck had been led on another fool's chase around the maze, and he was no nearer out than before—probably farther, if their working quarters were located away from the entrances, as seemed to be the case.

He moved back out of the light from the slit, and touched the switch. This time there was no denying that the little light bulb was glowing much more dimly than before. However, it gave enough illumination for him to read the dial on his oxygen tank. There were between fifteen and twenty minutes more to go on one tank—and the other was already empty.

He remembered the classical adage which advised a man who was faced with the inevitable to accept his fate gracefully; but he could also remember his father's comment on it:

"When you're at the end of your rope, you'll be a wise man to sit down and wait for the rope's end to hit you; but you'll live a lot longer if you grab it and start trying to climb up it, even if you don't know where it's tied."

There were three passages here. One led to the room where he'd first seen the chirper; the second was the one in which he was standing. Both were dead-end

streets. The third went off into nowhere—it might be
the nowhere that led out of the maze. He probably
couldn't make the ship unless it was the right exit, but
he could get close enough to scratch a warning in the
sand, with luck.

He turned down the third passage, no longer caring
about saving light or avoiding anything. His legs
pumped under him. The fear of dying came late, as if
the act of running had brought it out. It caught at his
chest, and made the air seem stale and re-used
already. His stomach wanted to turn over, but he had
no time. It was now or never.

The passage went on at a slow curve, and ended
in a double intersection. He chose one of the tunnels
at random and went racing down. It seemed to be
going upward slightly, although he couldn't be sure.
His fingers on the wall were already necessary to aid
the dying light of the little bulb, but he only tried to
run harder.

This time, when he saw the light, he knew better
than to hope; the hope came anyway, together with
another wave of fear—a mixture that left him no room
for reason. He dashed toward it frantically and came
to a stop beside another of the slits through the wall.

A bit of the scene inside told him he'd made a circle
right back to the workshop!

His mind was a crazy mixture of feelings. Part of
him was glad; it would mean that he would no longer
be a burden on the crew of the *Eros*. Part was worrying about his family and what they would have to
suffer because of his stowaway antics. But most of it

was shrieking against the idea of dying here uselessly, without even one friend to know what happened to him.

Then, as suddenly as the desperation of fear had hit him, it was gone. The relief left him weak and shaken, but he was master of himself again. He leaned against the slitted wall, breathing hard.

The valve on the tanks began to click back and forth, trying to turn on a new supply when there was none. He still had two or three minutes of air left— perhaps he could live on the stale air in his suit for a couple of minutes more.

"All right," he decided aloud. "Here goes nothing."

He brought his fist up against the slit and kicked at the door where the chirper had entered. He saw the creatures inside stir suddenly, but without any move toward the entrances. He kicked again, harder.

This time he got results. One of them got up and went to the entrance. He did something with his hands and it was open.

Chuck walked in, pushing the Martian aside, before its small round mouth could utter a sound. He stomped across the floor, heading toward the blower that was hanging on the wall. There was a chorus of chirps and shrieks around him, but he paid no attention to that. First things had to come first.

His hand was on the blower before they made a move toward him. Then it was the chirper who stood up and let out one of the soul-jarring shrieks that could tear the nerves out of anyone hearing it for the first time. Chuck shoved him aside and reached for the blower. His other hand was already on the slide that attached the oxygen tanks. He took one deep breath, and started to make the change-over.

The creatures hit him in a single wave that knocked the blower out of his hands and sent him tumbling to the floor. They couldn't hold him. On hands and knees, he crawled after the source of the oxygen his system demanded. The loosened tanks on his back came off under the pull of the Martians' hands and the air in the suit whooshed out suddenly.

He reached the blower in spite of them. He jerked to his feet, tossing several of them topsy-turvy. Everything was turning black, but he could feel the blower unit slide home and lock in place.

He pressed the switch and heard the welcome hum of the little unit at work. Then the second assault wave of Martians hit him.

Chapter 17 A Dying Race

CHUCK was half-unconscious as the Martians swarmed over him, and he was in no mood to struggle with them. The blower unit was purring along, sending air into his starved lungs, and there was no hurry about anything else. Of course, if they insisted on trying to tie him down, he wasn't going to help them. He . . .

He snapped out of it quickly, to find himself covered with creatures who were painstakingly trying to make him look like a mummy with something that reminded him of coarse thread. They had wound it wherever they could and were trying to reach new places.

He doubled his knees up sharply, slapping one little creature up against his chest; three others went tumbling backward as his legs snapped out again. It felt like a good way to warm up for better maneuvers, until they dragged out something long and nasty with sharp-pointed stones in it. Then he relaxed again, and let them tie him down to the floor. It began to look as if his idea that one human in a space suit was equal to fifty Martians wasn't as sound as it had seemed.

Chirper was playing an active part—at a safe distance. He jumped up and down, making violent gestures as he got new ideas for the others to follow. He chirped and chattered away with enough noise for a whole company. Now he stopped and surveyed the results, before deciding that Chuck was properly fastened down.

Then he let out a final screech and sprang forward, his hands going toward the blower unit. Chuck brought his arm around sideways and caught the Martian in the chest with his elbow, but the cords hampered him, and the blow lacked force. Chirper darted in behind him and made another grab for the blower.

The old Martian who had been trying to draw directions on the floor earlier had been watching the whole affair calmly. Now he came forward. One foot lifted from the floor and struck Chirper in the face in a neat stroke that sent the younger creature rolling across the floor. Before he could get to his feet, the old one's arms reached out and caught him by one leg and the back of his neck. Someone opened the entrance, and Chirper was thrown through it. The entrance closed again.

The old one came behind Chuck and examined the blower unit, making sure it was still seated properly in its slides. Evidently he realized its purpose, and didn't approve of killing Chuck at once. He walked back in front of the boy and touched his head.

"Sptz-Rrll," he announced, as nearly as Chuck could

hear. It was apparently his name or title, and Chuck pronounced his own name. The Martian clacked his teeth. "Tchkh!"

Chuck waited hopefully for further sign of friendship, but the old Martian stood quietly, simply staring at him, as if not sure what to do with this clumsy captive. It was an excellent time to use all the study of communication between races Chuck had made—but it couldn't be done while his hands were tied.

The eyes studied him a moment longer, and then Sptz-Rrll made a peculiar hunching motion of his body that must have been a shrug and turned back to the serious work that had occupied him before.

A maze of crude machinery leaned against the wall and Chuck could see that some of the parts were obviously of still clean and sparkling copper, as if they were tended daily, though most of them were now clearly useless. But the part the old creature was demonstrating now must have functioned more recently, though not in the memory of the younger ones.

Sptz-Rrll drew pictures on the dirt again. He picked up the copper gadget, put it down, and finally began taking it apart and reassembling it. Crude as it was in workmanship, the design was sound; it was a hand-tooled rotary impeller, meant to compress the air and drive it up a pipe that Sptz-Rrll indicated. Chuck followed the pipe upward to a small pile of stones covered with blackened bits of something.

The Martians had discovered fire, then. By compressing the air and forcing it through some vegetation, they had built themselves a crude forge for handling copper. Now Sptz-Rrll was telling them that it could be made to work again. He even brought out a few bits of metal from equipment that had probably broken or worn out long before.

The casing of the impeller was also ruined, so that the impeller could not work. Sometime in the past, a piece had been cracked open somehow. It had been hammered back into shape, but the crack remained, destroying its usefulness in compressing the thin air for their fire.

Sokolsky would have been interested, Chuck thought. He wondered whether Sokolsky would ever bother to remember that he had first discovered the secret of the canals with Chuck. Would any of them remember the seventh member of the crew if they got back to Moon City by determination and luck?

He'd been a fool to fight for a few hours more of life. What good would it do him? He was captured here, waiting for his battery to run down and lead to the same end, anyhow. Even if he broke free, there was still the maze of the tunnels with no opening from them that he could find. He might as well have gotten it all over with at once.

Then he grimaced at his own self-pity. At least he'd die knowing some of the answers to his questions. He'd wanted to find Martians, and he'd found them. In fact, he was the leading human expert on Martians. And a lot of good it amounted to.

Now activity was going on again, and his eyes followed it as a relief from his own thoughts. One of the younger Martians had pulled one of the bulky welders into the center of the room. With a great deal of manipulation, he managed to get a spark going and start the flame. While Sptz-Rrll watched, he began work on a broken bit of copper—using a stainless steel rod!

Sptz-Rrll studied the work for a minute more, and then jumped forward in disgust, making gestures that ended in the flame being extinguished and the welder returned to its position against the wall. It was easy to see now why the equipment had been stolen.

The old Martian had seen a chance to get back some of the culture that was rapidly dying away, and had seized it. Now, though, he was finding that all his hopes for fixing the ruined equipment were useless.

The sigh the old Martian made was almost human. He came over and stood in front of the boy again, holding the compressor in his hands. He thrust it toward Chuck doubtfully, and looked at the welder.

Chuck nodded, and wriggled his arms frantically, trying to show that they would have to be free. He saw understanding on Sptz-Rrll's face too.

But the old Martian only sighed again and turned back. He couldn't risk it. Chuck slumped down. For a moment, he had almost hoped. If he could get the welder in his hands, he'd have a weapon that would be strong enough to force them to map out a way to the surface!

The others in the workshop were going back to their jobs, molding clay, carving at stone utensils, or carefully trying to shape crude bits of copper. But Sptz-Rrll sat despondently in the center of the floor. He lifted a little stone lid there, and came up with a group of thin porcelain plates, all painted in bright colors.

Chuck strained his eyes toward them, and the old creature held them out. They were pictures of the work methods used in the past. The last one showed what might have been a windmill on the surface, with a shaft down to gearing that ran what could only have been the compressor. It was obvious that Mars had fought hard to develop civilization, but that the battle had been lost; they were on the long, downhill road back to savagery. After the windmill they had used the treadmill that still stood against the wall. Now they had nothing that needed power.

Chuck coughed harshly; his nose and throat had been bothering him. The cough only made things worse. He frowned, and then realized that the traces of water left in the blower unit for moistening the air must be gone; probably the Martians had drained that precious fluid off at once.

Sptz-Rrll was staring at him in deep thought now. The creature put the plates back slowly. He got up and moved back to a dark corner of the room. Then he approached Chuck again, hesitantly. He drew nearer, a step at a time, watching for a hostile move. Chuck sat motionlessly. Finally, Sptz-Rrll took the plunge. He darted in, and his quick little hands found the cap without error. Something gurgled, and the air grew more breathable. Sptz-Rrll screwed the cap back on, and again his eyes moved from Chuck to the welder.

Suddenly another weird cry broke from outside. One

by one, the Martians began to file from the room. Sptz-
Rrll waited until the last, but he obeyed whatever
command it was without holding up the parade. Chuck
was left alone in the workroom.

He muttered angrily, sure that the old Martian had
been about to risk freeing his hands in the hope he
would handle the welder. It was too late for that now.

He drew his arms up to his chest, testing the cords
without any real hope. He heaved—and the cords
snapped!

For a second he stared at them before he began
unwinding himself. They'd judged his muscles by his
size, not by his Earth origin, where he'd had to adapt
to nearly three times the effort that would be required
for the same results on Mars.

He slid out of the last of the cords and kicked them
aside. With a single jump he was across the room
and grabbing the big welding torch. He flicked it on,
setting the flame to low. Now let them try to stop
him! Even their ridiculous doors would be useless
against this.

The tanks were a full load for him, but he had
carried the equipment around while the ship was being
repaired, and he had no doubt of his ability to handle
it now. He let the flame spurt out with a roar and
brought it back to a clean, hot point again.

His step was almost jaunty as he headed toward
the entrance. There'd still be plenty of trouble—but
not if he walked into the first meeting room he'd seen
and gave them a real demonstration of a welder at
work. They'd be happy to get rid of him, then.

He passed the low bench where Sptz-Rrll had laid the ruined compressor. He picked it up and examined it, curious about the odd cleverness that had enabled them to find the best design for the housing and blades while they were still hammering it out of bits of copper by hand.

He knew he wasn't going to leave the old Martian without granting the request that had been in those big eyes. He'd never be able to sleep nights. From Sptz-Rrll's view, there had been no destruction or thievery; it had been a blinding hope for a rebirth of some of the culture they had once known, and the creature would have been a fool not to do anything he could to gain his ends. At least, there'd been no murdering involved.

Chuck found the right rod and adjusted his flame. He hadn't worked too much with copper, and he didn't like the idea. His experience had been with the hardest, toughest alloys known. But the equipment would braze copper, and he'd had some training. He spread the housing section on the floor and began depositing metal on it, smoothing it out as best he could. When it was done, he knew it was probably better than the original. One of the impeller blades was cracked off, and he found it among the broken bits Sptz-Rrll had been saving. It was a little more work to braze it back on, but it left the compressor as useful as it had been when it was first finished.

He felt better as he reassembled it and put it on the bench where the creature would be sure to find it. It had taken only a little time.

He glanced down at the indicator on the blower, at the thought of time. It should have been fully charged, but it wasn't. The Martians must have been fascinated by electrical equipment, judging by his burned-out helmet light and these batteries; probably they shorted them to watch the spark.

He had only an hour's current left. But it should be enough.

He turned to go, getting the welder ready to tackle the door, if it gave him trouble.

The door swung inward as he started toward it, and the Martians began trooping back!

Chuck lifted the torch and let the flame leap out. They halted at the sight, and he pointed it at the floor which steamed faintly, dry as it must have been. He pointed it toward them again and started forward.

They gave ground slightly, studying the situation out of their huge eyes, but without any sign of real fear. Here, on their home ground, the grab and run tactics they used on the surface were not even considered.

They drew backward, keeping as far to the side as they could, so that he had to watch every move they made. They were out of the workshop now, backing down the tunnel. Here the only light was from the torch, and it was a poor one. He'd been staring at it too intently—the plastic of his helmet could save him from the dangerous ultra-violet radiation of the torch, but it couldn't help his eyes adjust to both the bright spot of light and the shadows around.

The torch sputtered. It came on again, and again

it sputtered. This time it went out, leaving him in darkness. He'd forgotten to check the tanks and it had simply run out of fuel.

Knowing the reason didn't help him any. Knowing that whatever the Martians pilfered seemed to be about to stop working hadn't helped him, either.

He leaped backward toward the workshop, then reversed field, and plunged forward blindly into them. But it was a useless trick. Hands shot out toward him with the sureness of certain vision, and equally certain knowledge that he couldn't see. They piled onto him in a mad scramble, avoiding his flailing arms, and always beyond reach of his kicking legs.

A sudden shortness of breath warned him that they had found his vulnerable point. He stopped moving, before they shut off the blower intake completely. There was no use fighting when the other side had all the trumps.

Chuck let them walk him back into the workshop without any attempt to resist them. They chirped busily over the broken cords he had left, and reached a quick decision. Two of them began unfastening the straps of the welder harness, while three more came up with the unpleasant-looking weapon they had used to threaten him before.

He held out his hands without protest. The straps tightened on his wrists and were gathered neatly into a knot that he could not hope to work loose. Others took care of his legs.

This time there would be no breaking away. He'd played his best trick, and they'd beaten him.

Sptz-Rrll appeared finally, staring mournfully at the empty welder. His eyes were accusing, but the shrug he gave was the same as it had been before. The little Martian turned back to his bench.

He stopped, staring at the compressor, and a torrent of chirps came from his vocal cords, or whatever he used. Chuck's eyes narrowed as the Martians gathered around, examining the repaired mechanism. If they felt gratitude . . .

Sptz-Rrll put the compressor back on the table while the others returned to their work. The creature moved over to stare at the dial that indicated the charge remaining in Chuck's battery. A small hand came up over a round mouth, while the chest heaved and contorted, showing every symptom of strangling.

Then he shrugged and walked casually out the entrance.

Chapter 18 Martian Gesture

CHUCK pulled his knees up and dropped his helmet against them. In his ears, the faint whir of the blower made a background to his thoughts, reminding him of the minutes ticking away. It seemed that his whole life had been made up of minutes ticking away and reprieves that came to nothing. But this one hurt more than all the others.

Sptz-Rrll was only a Martian, and Chuck had been wrong in expecting human motivation of him; he knew that now. He'd read too much into mannerisms which might have had nothing to do with the emotions he'd believed them to mean. He'd been almost certain that the Martian would show gratitude in some way; he'd even begun to like the creature, even though he was a captive. To have his death dramatized and then shrugged off as unimportant . . .

Rule for understanding alien races: Don't read human feelings into nonhuman actions!

Sokolsky could probably have saved him the trouble of learning it the hard way. Sokolsky would have gone off on a long lecture on the subject.

Sptz-Rrll came back as casually as he had left, carrying a heavy porcelain plate in his hands. The others
immediately dropped what they were doing to cluster
around, with soft twitting and chirping noises. Then
the old Martian came over toward Chuck and bent
down to begin unfastening his bonds!

For the second time in one minute, Chuck cursed
his own foolishness. He'd been making up a rule—
which he violated while he thought of it; he'd been
taking it for granted that the first interpretation of
Sptz-Rrll's shrugging gesture had been the only possible one, because it seemed completely human.

Or was he still misinterpreting, and not being freed,
after all?

The Martian put an end to that worry almost at
once. He squatted on the floor and drew a square,
waving his hand around the workshop to indicate that
it was being symbolized. A series of zigzag lines followed. At the other end, there was a crude sketch
of the space ship.

Sptz-Rrll stood up then and reached for one of
Chuck's hands. Without more ceremony, he headed
for the entrance which opened at once. Five of the
other Martians followed as they moved into the dark-
ened tunnels; each of them carried one of the illuminating squares Chuck had seen on the walls.

The squares gave off only a dim, weak light, but
it was enough for him to see. The way was twisting,
as they struck down side passages, through straight
sections and curves, and seemed to wander aimlessly.
It was probably exactly as Sptz-Rrll had drawn it, and

he had no reason to doubt that it was the shortest route to the ship.

He wondered whether they had known of his wanderings around the tunnels before? If they had, why hadn't they made an earlier effort to capture him? He tried to find some way to ask it of the Martian, but it was too complicated.

A screech sounded from behind them, and the procession stopped until another Martian could catch up with them. The lamp for Chuck's helmet was in its hands, and it extended the useless object to him gravely. It was not so useless at that, he realized. There'd be fresh batteries on the ship. He took it with an attempt at equal formality and inserted it into the catches on his helmet.

They must have known of his stumbling around; the helmet was a giveaway to that. Then he realized that there were seven of the Martians with him—the same number as the crew of the *Eros*. It might be sheer coincidence, or it might mean they were accompanying him with the idea of meeting more of the crew.

There would be mysteries for years to come. Man had never been fully able to understand different customs among various groups of his own people. How could complete understanding be achieved with a race which grew up under such utterly different conditions?

Maybe they were going to act as a formal dickering group to get the best price for the return of the equipment the ship needed—if they'd consent to give them up after having spent so much trouble to accumulate all the gadgets they wanted.

They passed an open door, and an arm slipped out, quickly dropping Chuck's knife into his hand. That arm had been covered with a silvery coating of fur, totally unlike those of all the Martians Chuck had seen.

There were too many unsettled things to worry about such mysteries, or to let him feel particularly happy. Strangely, his deepest pleasure was not at being returned safely to the ship, but at finding that Sptz-Rrll had been all that he had believed.

They were on an inclined ramp now, moving upward. Chuck couldn't tell whether it was the one on which he had come down, but there was something vaguely familiar about it. He kept looking around for something familiar, but there was nothing he could identify.

Sptz-Rrll reached for one of the illuminating squares and moved it close to the floor, pointing. There were the dim prints of Chuck's boots there. Apparently the Martian had interpreted his glances correctly and was reassuring him.

They came up through the same mosaic pattern that had first shown Chuck the way down, into late afternoon sunlight. The boy realized that less than twenty-four hours had gone by.

The seven Martians dropped back to let him lead the way. He stopped, though, for another look at the mosaic. The silhouettes of the humanoids on it were crudely done, but they gave enough details, if all were studied, to show that the race had changed very little since the floor was laid. Chuck wondered if there were records or legends that went back to the

time when they had lived on the surface, before they
found a refuge from the extremes of Martian temperature by going underground?

Sptz-Rrll tugged at his hand, pointing to the indicator that showed the charge of the blower battery
was almost exhausted.

Chuck shook himself. The Martian was right—he
had no business lingering here while his battery ran
down. He began a quick lope toward the ship. He'd
have to go ahead and warn the ship that the Martians were coming if he could make Sptz-Rrll understand that it would be better to wait.

The Martian caught his hand again, and pointed
to the blower. He made a fast whirl of his hand in
a roughly circular motion, then went slower and
slower, to follow it with his strangling gestures.

The sprint had taken more out of Chuck than it
should have done. But he had to make it to the ship.

Two of the Martians gravely reached for his legs,
two more tried to take his arms, and another pair were
linking hands around his middle. Sptz-Rrll was motioning toward the helmet. With a quick, well-coördinated
motion, they had him stretched out horizontally,
and were carrying him—giving him a chance to
rest and get by with the smaller amount of air the
motor could pump in now.

They came over the top of the dune toward the
ship and into full view of the whole ship's crew. Chuck
could barely see them, at the angle of his head. He
tried to wave an arm, but it was securely held by one
of the Martians.

The men were facing toward the procession now. Vance's hand went for his automatic, and the metal of it flashed bluely in the sunlight. Chuck groaned. But the little form of Sokolsky had leaped in the way of the shot, motioning frantically.

A second later, the doctor was running toward them, his face a picture of misery. Then his eyes fell on Chuck's smile, and his own expression underwent a lightning change. His mouth opened and shut, shouting out the news over the radio to those who were watching.

Sptz-Rrll motioned to the indicator as the doctor bent over, and Sokolsky fell into a trot beside them, touching helmets. "We thought they'd captured you and killed you—that this was some kind of funeral procession. But I had to be sure before we gummed up the works. What gives?"

"They're friendly—they let me go."

Steele came bounding toward them, waving a new battery, and Chuck motioned his bearers to put him down. He changed batteries quickly, then touched helmets. "Get me a radio," he explained tersely, and headed for the ship.

It was a sloppy job of installation, but a quick one. He came out again, to find the Martians waiting quietly, while the men stared at them. Only Sokolsky seemed happy about having the Martians around; the others were filled with the worry and suspicion they had picked up from sad experience.

One of the younger ones was watching Sokolsky apparently trying to burrow into the sand. Suddenly, the young Martian made a wiggling dive and began to melt from sight. There was a little ripple on the surface, and he came up at Sokolsky's back, chirping busily. The doctor laughed as the Martian shook himself, sending a cloud of dust flying.

Vance cut through the chatter. "We'll hear your story later, Chuck—I gather you're in their good graces. But how much can we trust them? And is there any chance we can get back the stuff they stole from us?"

"Your answer is already coming up the dune," Sokolsky told him quickly.

They turned to see a procession of more than fifty Martians drawing near. Some were carrying the welders, others were burdened with a miscellaneous collection. One, Chuck noticed, held four cans—the missing corned beef, including the can that had been dropped in the tunnel. Sptz-Rrll tapped the welding tanks and made an elaborate ritual of the gesture which Chuck had considered a shrug. From one of the Martians, he took a small handful of bits of broken copper and offered them to the boy.

"Take them," Sokolsky advised. "This seems to be a typical culture of its kind; formality and high-dignity are the big things. And we'd all better start thinking of them as men or Martians, if we're going to get along well—no more of this 'humanoid' business, or we'll find ourselves looking down on them, and that won't go."

Dick Steele came over. "And somebody might offer some food to Chuck—it's considered good manners in our society. Come on, kid. We've been on short rations, but I think we can rustle up some decent food for you."

Sokolsky waved them off, and turned back to the young Martian. Chuck looked doubtfully at Sptz-Rrll, but he knew the Martians had been on board the ship without invitation. He gestured, and the three of them headed through the air lock. There was no sign that the heavy air or high temperature bothered the Martian, except that his coat suddenly flattened down against his skin.

"It isn't so good, Chuck," Dick told the boy as he began pulling food out of the galley and setting it out in the mess hall. "Even Vance has had to admit that with everything, we can't make the return trip. We can't do it, even with all the stuff returned to us. Even getting the winches back—which we can't, naturally—wouldn't help much. We're stuck—and we're down to two meals a day, without much then."

The engineer held out some of the food toward the Martian, who shoved it aside politely. "Anybody who expects to survive better learn to eat sand. Go ahead and eat—you need it. None of us wanted to eat much since you disappeared."

He took out a pencil and some paper and began drawing a diagram of the solar system. Then he tossed it aside. "It's easier to do this outside, where I can point the sun out. I might as well let your friend know where we're from."

Sptz-Rrll reached out inquiringly for the pencil and paper. He chattered his teeth together as he saw the marks that it made, and began drawing busily, while Chuck tried to tell about the things that had happened to him.

The Martian interrupted, offering the pad to Chuck. Crude as all Martian drawing seemed to be, it was easy enough to follow. The first showed a diagram of the Martians turning the space ship over, with another below it showing them pouring acid over the winches. Sptz-Rrll again went through his shrugging gesture, which apparently had something to do with an apology. He turned the page over.

This time the ship was drawn part way toward the vertical, with ropes leading back toward a whole horde of the Martians. Other Martians were busily digging out a hole for it, and still others were swarming all over the ship while seven rather strange-looking humans stood by and watched.

He handed it to Dick, who looked it over quickly, with a surprised expression that gradually changed to a wide smile. The engineer picked up the pencil and made a series of rapid strokes beside the big picture; in almost exact imitation of the style the Martian had used, there was a procession of Martians going back from the ship, carrying goods of various kinds.

"We'll have to get Vance's okay," he told Chuck quietly. "But it would work. With unlimited labor, even unskilled labor that can't speak our language, we could make it with time to spare. And we have plenty of things they can use."

That night, the floodlights had been brought out from the ship and were directed at a wide spot on the sand near by. Seven men from Earth and seven others from Mars were busily at work, tracing patterns in the sand and wiping them out. They were also using signs which increased as they went along; there was no attempt to organize a common language yet, but one was growing into existence there, all the same.

Vance grinned at Chuck, who sat across from Sptz-Rrll. "I guess I'll get used to the fact that you're acting captain, Chuck, while they're around. I'm not sure but what I like it—you'll have to do all the settling of disagreements between the two groups."

"He won't have any trouble from the Martians," Sokolsky said. "Not until we get them so civilized that their own natural culture goes to pieces, and not then, if we go at it right. These people regard friendship as an absolute, all-out thing."

Chuck nodded. They'd already proved that. Once Chuck had helped them with the welding, they were compelled to risk their lives, if necessary, for him and for his people, according to their codes.

It would require constant vigilance to make sure that only the highest type people from Earth came in contact with them, but the United Nations was set up now to handle such situations, even in cases of national trusteeships and planets beyond the Earth.

Things would work out, he was sure. Earth could give Mars the metal and the power needed, and some of the Martian plants would pay for all the trouble, with more than equal value. Both cultures could become richer because of the relationship. Men from Earth and men from Mars could rise together—some day even to the stars that filled the sky overhead.

But all that was in the background of his mind. In the foreground, he knew that he was no longer worried about having been a seventh man on the ship. He'd finally earned his way. He no longer cared whether he was a man or a boy—and maybe that was what being a man meant.

He leaned back on the sands, looking up at the *Eros,* which would soon be going back to the Moon. There'd be more trips after that return. Discovery of life and intelligence here had made that certain.

On the next trip there'd be no trouble. He was eighteen now, and he was experienced. He knew he'd be back.